Peach Blossom Hollow

D1610613

PEACH BLOSSOM HOLLOW

A SWEET FRIENDS TO LOVERS ROMANCE

HOCKEY SWEETHEARTS

JEAN ORAM

Peach Blossom Hollow
by Jean Oram
Copyright © 2022 Jean Oram
All rights reserved.
First Large Print Edition

Printed in the United States of America unless otherwise stated on the last page of this book. Published by Oram Productions Alberta, Canada.

Cover design by Jean Oram

Complete cataloguing information available online or upon request.

Oram, Jean.

Peach Blossom Hollow: A Sweet Friends to Lovers Romance / Jean Oram.—1st. ed.

ISBN: 978-1-990833-33-5, 978-1-990833-36-6 (paperback), 978-1-990833-35-9 (large print)

First Oram Productions Large Print Edition: November 2022

CHAPTER 1

*V*iolet Granger pushed on the changing room door with her cumbersome costumed hands. *Locked.* She angled her head back to aim the costume's eye holes at the number on the door. She'd left her street clothes in an even-numbered room.

At least she was pretty certain she had. After an hour of running around out in the hockey arena to get used to the bulky green and black dragon costume, she was a sweaty, frustrated mess.

Tempted to pull off the massive head so she could see and breathe better—even though that was supposedly forbidden outside the changing room—she waddled farther down the hallway, her dragon tail wagging after her.

She'd nearly died approximately five and a half times during this first in-costume practice out in the stands. The Dragons NHL team was in the process of hiring her a handler—which until today she hadn't believed she'd truly need. But after falling down steps, getting her tail caught in elevator doors and knocking into the rows of seating, she was fully on board with enlisting as many handlers as possible so she wouldn't make the news by dying in a dragon costume during a live NHL game.

Although maybe that would finally get Owen Lancaster's attention.

She snorted. No. No thinking about Owen. She was over him. Stupid one-sided crush and his revived major league baseball career taking him away from Sweetheart Creek—and her. She'd finally felt she was getting somewhere with her shy flirting. And then he'd left.

Men always left—whether she was close to summoning the courage to ask one out, or they were standing at the altar about to say "I do." Or, in her ex-fiancé's case, "I don't."

This costume was part of a plan. An important, break-the-curse and heal her spirit kind of plan.

But the curse... Her grandmother had been left with three young toddlers in Korea when her husband announced he was going to Hollywood, and that it was no place for a nice Korean woman.

Then, years later, Violet's mother had been left by *her* husband when a beautiful younger version had come along. A singer. Bold and gregarious. Loved to entertain.

Very unlike her loyal, quiet mom.

Violet herself had been left enough times to know she had to do something different—had to *be* someone different—in order to change the fate that had been handed to her by some cranky Korean gods her great-grandmother had allegedly snubbed by running away instead of accepting the husband chosen for her by her community.

And no, none of the woman in her family had given their partner a pair of shoes, which was a Korean superstition. Give them shoes, watch them run away from you. Although Violet wondered if there was an opposite superstition her mom hadn't told her about. Maybe one where you gave your partner something like an anchor to make them stay.

But this dragon costume? It was a method, according to an online pop psychologist, to help Violet break out of her shyness in a safe way. She hadn't always been this timid, but having love smack her down enough times... Well, a part of her spirit had just given up on her.

So to be different, she had to act different. Become different through action. With her new job as a mascot she was placing herself in a situation where she *had* to be gregarious and goofy, playing to the team's fans. Wearing the costume would reacclimatize her to being the woman she once was, one not afraid of putting herself out there.

There would be no more locked jaw due to shyness. She would be free. And able to talk to hunky men.

Then she'd find love.

She'd show the curse she couldn't be broken. She'd win. She'd break *it*.

And there were plenty of men here in this arena to test her new theory out on.

Potential love matches? Statistically, there had to be several.

Violet stopped in front of the next even-numbered locker room door.

Bliss. That's what it would feel like to push her sweat-soaked hair off her forehead and out of her eyes. She'd feel so light and comfortable in her street clothes.

She placed her hands on the green door and inhaled. Oh, to have a refreshing shower and a nice long drink of cool water.

She pushed against the door. It opened an inch, then shut again. Violet let out a frustrated growl and heaved her entire five-foot-two-inch frame against the freshly painted metal. This time it gave easily, sending her flailing forward into the room, tripping on her large dragon feet and then plowing into a figure that stood between her and the cinderblock wall just beyond.

She landed face-first, her costume head sliding up and off as gravity tugged her downward. The man grabbed for her while she twisted, struggling to get her feet under her as the door banged against her leg. As Violet slid to the floor between the wall and a giant hockey bag she caught a glimpse of what she was certain were naked torsos and men in boxer shorts.

Wrong room.

The floor smelled like used hockey equipment. But lovely music filled the air. A nice relaxing tune.

Splayed on her back, Violet closed her eyes,

wishing her dragon head hadn't come off in her tumble.

Worst day ever.

"Are you okay?" asked the man she'd fallen against.

Why had she taken this job?

Why had she decided she needed to push her way out of being who she'd become over the last two years? A quiet nobody shuffling papers for Mayor Nestner. That had been safe. It had been fine. Lonely, and not particularly exciting, unless the town armadillo, Bill, caused mischief and someone came to the mayor about it. But the job had been okay.

With a sigh she cracked one eyelid open, letting the man fussing over her come into focus. Hockey player. Kneeling. Looking concerned. His two front teeth were slightly crooked and he had kind, dark blue eyes. He was fresh-faced, ready to get onto the ice for practice.

And she was a sweaty mess. Violet scrunched her eyes shut again, wanting to pretend she was dead.

"Are you okay?" he repeated.

She swallowed hard, glancing up at him again. She knew this guy. Okay, she didn't *know* him, but knew *of* him. Leo Pattra, former bull riding champion who was now playing in the National Hockey League, like switching professional sports was something people did all the time. He was a sweet, hunky hottie she'd be absolutely tongue-tied around should they ever meet.

And they were meeting.

He was standing over her, looking more and more concerned the longer she remained silent.

Maybe she could will herself to pass out until it was all over?

Violet sighed and tried to sit up, but her large dragon belly made it impossible to fold forward. She attempted to roll onto her side, but found herself wedged between the bag and the wall. She flopped back again, feeling like an upside-down turtle.

"Need help?" Leo asked, watching her with those lovely eyes. He held out his hand, but with her giant dragon-clawed paws she knew she couldn't grasp it. Nor could she push her bangs out of her eyes so she could see better.

Maybe she could will herself to disappear, like how she'd pretended she was invisible when she was a kid.

Just close your eyes. Ignore the hunky man.

"I'm Leo."

Yeah, pretending to be invisible hadn't worked

when she was a kid, either. Just resulted in a lot of teasing.

"Dezzie." She blinked. "Dragons' mascot." Her voice had worked. She glanced back at Leo, then away. Maybe this costume acclimation idea wasn't so bad, after all.

He smiled. "What's your real name? And *are* you okay?" Carefully, still kneeling beside her, he peeled her sweat-plastered hair off her forehead and away from her eyes.

This would be a great time to disappear because…ew. Could she be any more disgusting?

That familiar shyness burned through her, locking down her ability to meet his eyes or speak. He was too cute. Too kind. Too caring.

Too close.

And he didn't seem to mind her sweat-plastered hair.

Heartbreaker.

"You have a very pretty face," he said gently. Without warning, he gripped her arms through the costume's thick fabric like a seasoned livestock wrangler. Tingles zipped along her skin as if he'd electrocuted her, and for a moment she thought she'd broken something. Then she realized it was just the power of Hunky-hunk, who was now rolling to his heels with athletic ease, fluidly lifting himself onto his feet and pulling her along.

Yum. She loved a strong man. And one who gave her compliments was even better.

There was no chance she'd be able to speak to him. Ever. At all. Pop-psych couldn't work on everything.

Feeling more eyes on her, she glanced over her shoulder. The locker room was full of curious, half-dressed San Antonio Dragons.

This would be a fantastic time for that invisibility thing to finally work.

Leo Pattra had no idea who the woman in the dragon costume was, but she was cute. And she was obviously mortified at the way she'd fallen into a room filled with half-dressed players. He scooped up her dragon head and steered her back into the hallway.

"I'm Leo," he said again, hoping she'd introduce herself as something other than the mascot. He didn't have time to get tangled up in flirting or dating at the moment, but this shy gal in the gigantic, wingless dragon costume had him intrigued. If he was the type to fall in love for the sheer joy of it rather than the old-fashioned reason of needing a life partner, she might be someone he'd consider. Even though she seemed way too bashful for her own good.

Anyway, it didn't matter. He needed a partner. Someone to help him further his career, make bank so he'd never have to worry about how he was going to feed his future kids, and then retire soon after that so he could enjoy that family. The way he figured it, he needed someone like Christine Lagrée, a donor relations manager for the Special Olympics, to see him, help him, marry him. She did an amazing job of being someone to follow on social media, and mutual friends had told him she frequently received lucrative job offers.

He sighed, almost missing it when the mascot murmured, "Violet."

"Nice to meet you."

When she didn't reply, he added, "And you're Dezzie this season?"

She gave him a dry look, surprising him, and his intrigue ratcheted up a notch.

"I know, stupid question," he admitted, wishing she'd give him a full-sentence reply. He felt as though getting one would be a triumph. "I'm new this year."

He repressed the urge to explain why, at twenty-seven—the average NHL players' age—he was just a rookie.

Unlike most players, he hadn't toiled for eons in the minors, waiting to be called up. He'd actually spent several years as a professional bull rider before deciding to change to a less dangerous career.

However, he figured most people assumed that being a rookie at his age meant he'd been passed up for a decade, and so wasn't really that great at playing right wing.

"I take it you went in the wrong room?" he said, glancing down the hallway.

She mumbled something about an even-numbered door.

Leo hustled forward, heading to the next room. Number six. Locked.

Violet heaved a sigh. She looked exhausted and sweaty.

Voices filtered down the hall and Nuvella, one of the two main mucky-mucks on the PR team, appeared around a corner. When she spotted Violet her back straightened and she quickened her stride.

Violet reached for him. Leo opened his arms for a hug before realizing she wanted her dragon head, and that her eyes were filled with panic. Wow, he was sorely out of practice hanging out with the opposite sex.

"I can carry it," he said as he allowed her to snatch it from him. She fumbled it in her clawed hands before managing to get it back on.

"Violet!" Nuvella called, hustling toward them. She had bleached-white hair, offset by bright red lipstick slashed across her tight mouth. "You can't be seen outside the changing rooms without your head. We were *very* clear on that."

"She fell," Leo said, angling himself between Violet and the Cruella de Vil wannabe. "She couldn't get up and she needs a helper. She can't see in this costume and it's a hazard."

"We're working on it, *Leo*," Nuvella snapped. She pointed at Violet. "The head stays on no matter what. What if a child saw a headless Dezzie?"

"She needs help," Leo said firmly.

"I *know*."

He kept his gaze on the woman even as he guided Violet farther down the hall, away from her. Once they were alone again, he said, "The evil witch from the west is gone."

He'd had some meetings with Nuvella and her colleague, Mark, and the one word he'd use to describe them and their cluelessness about hockey? *Alarming.*

Violet raised her big paws, gave a little na-na wave, then spun around and waggled her giant butt in the direction Nuvella had gone. Leo laughed and shushed her, even though she hadn't made a sound. The new PR twins from New York —The Twins, as everyone called them—weren't making many friends, and he wondered how long they'd last. But in the meantime, they had to play nice.

"You're going to be a hit with the audience," Leo told Violet as he pushed on the next door. It opened. A small duffel bag and a water bottle sat on one of the wooden benches. "I think this is you."

Violet shuffled forward, reaching up as though eager to pull off her dragon head the moment she crossed the threshold. Leo held the door wide for her, and sure enough, she popped it off with a loud exhale. She rewarded him with a tiny smile as she waddled into the room, whacking him in the shins with her swinging tail.

She placed the head on a bench and reached behind her with those costumed hands, struggling to grip the zipper.

He hurried to assist her, hoping she was

wearing something decent underneath, and that he wouldn't get brought up on charges for trying to be helpful. He had a plan for this year and avoiding all scandals was top of the list.

Not that he was prone to trouble, but if he wanted the kind of sponsorship deal he could retire on, he needed to stay squeaky clean. And undressing the pretty mascot might not land him in the squeaky-clean camp.

He hesitated before releasing the zipper. "Do you mind if I help you out of this? Or is Cruella de Vil coming back to turn you into a coat?"

To his surprise, Violet let out a laugh that filled the room.

"These are attached," she said, looking over her shoulder and waggling her enormous clawed, green-and-black paws. "Please free me."

He pulled the zipper tab down to her hips, holding the costume closed at the neckline with his other hand for modesty's sake. "How did you get into this thing?"

She turned to face him, and he released his grip. "Magic."

"I'll say." The neck was so tight she couldn't have wriggled her way in. She must have had someone zip her up. "When will they find you some help?"

She shrugged, meeting his gaze briefly. Her face was turning red, and he could see shyness zipping her up like a reverse of the costume he'd just freed her from. Leo didn't want her clamming up again. He wanted to know more about this reserved, slightly sassy woman who'd crashed into him.

"Do you like the job?" he asked.

"It's fun," she admitted, her eyes lighting up.

"And?"

"Exhausting."

"Yeah?"

"I had no idea I could sweat so much."

He smiled. A full sentence. It *was* possible.

And they said nice guys finish last.

"It looks like you worked hard," he said, gesturing to her damp hair.

The big dragon paws swept to her straight black hair, and she ducked as though trying to hide.

"You're how I look when I get off the ice," he said with a chuckle. "The things we do for hockey, huh?"

She lifted a shoulder in a half shrug.

"If you'd asked me when I was sixteen if this is where I was going to end up..."

She laughed again, the sound light this time,

carefree, then looked confused. "You didn't always want the NHL?"

"Most hockey players have worked toward this forever. I've taken a few detours."

She nodded, watching him with unreadable eyes before reaching for the pink water bottle on the bench with her padded hands—knocking it over. She gave a resigned shrug, sending the costume slipping from her shoulders like a curtain dropping, revealing her petite body. She was wearing a pink tank top and tight, stretchy black shorts.

With the costume bunched around her ankles, her hands now free, she reached for the water bottle, tipped her head back and took several long, unladylike gulps.

After a final swallow, she glanced at him again with those intriguing, almost-black eyes.

"Sorry," he said, stepping back toward the door. "I should let you do your thing." He stopped, thinking about how dangerous it was for her to run around in the costume without a guide. She needed somebody. Soon. And someone who would take good care of her. Not a random stranger.

"They seriously let you out there without a handler?"

"I was impatient to learn the ropes."

He paused, mulling over the fact that she'd spoken another full sentence—a win for him.

Leo's sense of duty was rearing up in him. Was it because she was shy, or petite, or that she had tumbled into him that he felt the need to look out for her?

If she fell in here, alone, who knew how long she'd roll around, unable to get up, helpless as she waited for someone to find her?

His mom was always nagging him to let people take care of their own business.

He nodded once, then grabbed the door handle.

But what if Cruella hired someone who didn't care? Who didn't read the crowd properly? Who couldn't protect the woman wearing the costume? People sometimes got aggressive with mascots, not knowing who was inside.

And what if they hired a man, and he didn't avert his eyes when he helped Violet out of her Dezzie outfit?

"You should ask them to hire a friend," Leo suggested. "It'll make it more fun, and nobody looks out for you the way a friend will."

Preferably she had a big burly one who was already married.

"Actually…" Violet said slowly, focusing on the wall as an idea seemed to hit her. She grinned. "Actually, someone promised she'd take the handler job if I became mascot. She was only teasing, but…"

"You should hold her to that promise."

Violet's smile turned crafty, but her voice was sweet and clear as she said, "I think I *will* hold her to that promise, Leo."

CHAPTER 2

"*H*e what?" Violet asked, horrified that her reply came out as a squeak.

Her friend Daisy-Mae Ray showed the photo on her phone.

Married.

Owen Lancaster, her old crush, had gotten married. He'd left town—and her—in order to return to major league baseball. Not even a year had passed, and he was already married?

Her ex-fiancé, who'd moved to a new town when she'd refused to budge from Sweetheart Creek after their humiliating wedding fiasco, was engaged again, as well.

She seriously needed to get busy with that blasted curse.

Be different, act different.

Staring at Owen's happy wedding photo, Violet felt as if all the sweet guys, like Leo Pattra, would never notice her—not as a woman worthy of dating. Nobody would.

She sank onto the bench, her Dragon costume pushing up around her, almost swallowing her.

"I'm sorry," Daisy-Mae whispered. "I thought you'd want to know."

Violet made a gurgling sound.

Her friend's voice grew sympathetic. "It seemed like the two of you were going to…"

"I know," Violet said quickly. She didn't need to hear it. She and Owen… It had felt as though they had a special connection. When they'd met, he was fresh out of the league, and she'd been left at the altar. They'd shared the pain of crushed dreams. It had taken them a while to edge toward flirting. Then to dance around the idea of dating.

It had all felt so certain. Intentionally slow and careful. A rebuilding of her confidence, a second chance to break the curse.

Or so she'd thought.

Violet hadn't predicted that he'd leave so suddenly, returning to baseball and, obviously, his ex-girlfriend.

But here she was—still single, and wondering what had happened.

Violet's shyness had grown worse after Wyatt and the altar abandonment. But it had become debilitating after Owen left without even a goodbye.

"I'm never going to find someone," she said with a sigh. It was too hard, overcoming her fears and getting back up again after falling flat on her face in front of everyone she loved.

"No, remember? We're two single gals out on the town!" Daisy-Mae gave her an encouraging nudge. "Dragon Babes! We're putting ourselves out there so we *can* find love."

When Daisy-Mae landed the job as her handler a few days ago, Violet had insisted they live it up as a Dragon babe duo. They were ready to meet hunky men, and what better way than through their jobs, and being in the big city on their work nights?

But Violet had a sneaking suspicion that despite her best plans and wishes for a great season out on the town, her best friend would soon be up to her eyeballs in dates, and their duo idea would fade away. That suspicion had grown into full-blown worry this afternoon as they'd worked on her mascot moves in the stands during the team's practice. Daisy-Mae, as usual, was done up like a Texas babe, and it had practically brought the entire rink of men to a standstill. Tall, blonde, and with a traffic-stopping smile, she was a deadly package in a tight short shirt and shorts.

"I can't see much through these eyeholes—" Violet patted her costume head "—but it's clear you're going to remain single for approximately zero seconds once the Dragons find a way to meet you off the ice."

Which meant her Dragon Babes plan better come with a Single and Lonely Violet backup plan. And it should probably involve therapy.

"Hey, are you okay?" Daisy-Mae crouched in front of her. They'd had fun out in the stands, and Violet had been silly in the costume, feeling freer than if she'd been hanging out with family or friends. But now reality returned, nipping at her heels, reminding her that she wasn't outgoing or desirable.

"Yeah, fine." She stood and turned her back to her friend. "Unzip me?"

"This guy asked if you're single."

Unable to stop herself, Violet spun around again. "Really? Who?"

Despite the vibe she'd gotten from Leo, that he was just looking for a friend, she couldn't help but hope that Daisy-Mae was going to say his name.

Her friend shrugged. "He's the unassuming type of cute."

"Trouble?"

She laughed. "Aren't they all?"

"Double date?"

"You're on." Daisy-Mae headed for the door. "I'll see if I can catch him." She winked and was gone.

Violet's heart hammered. She knew Daisy-Mae was going to find love this season. And for the first time, even though she knew she was acting like an ever-hopeful preteen about to get her world crushed again, she felt there might be a chance for her, too.

* * *

The first week of October, Leo scanned the conference room, looking for a familiar face as he smoothed his name tag over his shirt's pocket. He spotted a few guys from the team, several strangers in suits, and a woman he hadn't stopped thinking about since she'd literally crashed into the Dragons' locker room a week ago. Violet.

He weaved his way among the tables, nodding or tipping his cowboy hat to people he passed. He liked that the new-employee orientation included everyone in the organization, from players to office types to ticket sales agents. It made him feel he was part of something bigger than just the team of athletes. And it reminded him that his performance impacted a lot of careers besides his own.

He paused at a table for three near the front of the conference room. "Fancy meeting you here," he said to Violet. She was seated beside the woman he recognized as her new handler. "Anyone sitting here?"

Violet immediately turned red, while the blonde gave him an enormous smile and gestured to the vacant spot.

"Be our guest." She reached across Violet to shake his hand after he sat and removed his hat. "I'm—"

"Daisy-Mae, right? You're Violet's helper and handler?"

"Smart cookie."

"Not really." He pointed to her name tag,

noting that she'd chosen a Daffy Duck sticker for her name tag. Violet had chosen a Yosemite Sam for her black-and-white sweater, same as him. "But I do think you'll have your hands full keeping this one from falling down the steps of the stands." He winked at Violet, and the shade of red deepened.

"Tell me about it!" Daisy-Mae said with a laugh.

"Hi," Leo said to Violet. He'd managed to get a complete sentence out of her when they'd met, and now it looked like he was back at square one. And not because of the teasing. He got the feeling she didn't mind.

Realizing he'd become distracted by Violet's shyness and had forgotten to introduce himself to Daisy-Mae, he said, "I'm sorry, I'm—"

"Leo Pattra." Daisy-Mae shot him a triumphant smile. "And I didn't have to read your name tag."

She'd heard of him? He glanced at Violet, who was still blushing. He liked the implications that she may have mentioned him to her friend.

Although, as he had learned during his bull riding days, people often knew of him and his career before they actually met him in person. But despite Violet being obviously far from his type, he liked the idea of her talking about him.

"Your parents have a sense of humor?" Violet asked quietly.

"Sorry? Oh, my name? Yeah. Sort of." He'd received his fair share of teasing for the way his name rhymed with Cleopatra.

"History buffs?" she suggested.

"No, just liked the way it sounded."

"Are they proud you're a hockey player?"

"Mom's worried I'll lose my front teeth." She definitely preferred hockey over bull riding, though. There was a lower risk for paralyzation, for one. "And she says I already have enough belt buckles to last a lifetime. So…" He gave a shrug, proud of how casually he'd slipped in the fact that he'd won a lot of awards in his rodeo event.

"Do yours think it's cool you're the mascot?" he asked.

Violet rolled her eyes and gave him that same dry look she had the other day. It tickled him as much as it had the first time.

One word to describe her: *shy.*

No, *enigma.*

Sassy?

Maybe *intriguing.*

He might need several words for a woman like her.

"Vi's mom had a coronary when she found out she'd taken this job," her friend interjected.

"No, she didn't. But almost." Violet's voice was slightly scolding, but her eyes sparkled with a hint of mischief.

"Her mom wanted her to be an accountant, lawyer or mutual fund manager," Daisy-Mae added.

"Good thing she's in Korea for the foreseeable future," Violet muttered.

"Korea? Wow."

"She moved back to take care of her mom," Daisy-Mae explained for Violet. "She grew up there, but hated it so never taught Vi anything cool like how to swear in Korean."

"How about your dad?" Leo asked Violet. "Did he go too?"

She waved away the question and he sized her up, trying to figure her out. She was serious and self-conscious, but she had a goofy side and seemed to be willing to go against family expectations.

The employee orientation session began, and after HR's quick spiel about reading the manuals that were being passed out, the team's owner, Miranda Fairchild, gave a brief presentation about the new charity. The charity would raise funds, brighten the lives of patients at the local children's hospital with a few hockey player visits, and the like.

Leo sat forward. Something like this was totally up his alley, and might help him get on the radar for a sponsorship deal with a company like Family Zone. The company had theme parks and even movies and TV shows. It was a huge company, and he loved everything about them.

"This is really cool," he whispered to Violet. She nodded, and he noticed she was leaning forward, too. "I'll join if you do."

When she glanced at him in surprise, he lifted his brows, challenging her.

Her hand shot up, and Miranda nodded at her.

"Will anyone be going as Dezzie?" Violet asked.

"You're welcome to, of course. I think the kids would love to meet our favorite dragon."

Violet sat taller, then gave Leo a pointed look of her own.

"Where do we sign up?" he called out.

Miranda smiled, looking almost relieved. "Thanks, Leo. I'll mark you down."

A few more volunteers came forward and Miranda sent a sign-up form around the room.

"I love kids," Violet stated.

"Yeah, me too. They're fun."

"I want about a half dozen."

Leo laughed. "For real?"

"In theory. But in terms of practicality, somewhere between one and three."

"Those are good numbers. But my vote will always be for more than one."

"Being an only sucks."

Leo thought about what it would be like to be without his three siblings. He couldn't imagine it.

"You can approach me at any time about the charity," Miranda continued. "That includes family and friends, as we're not exclusive to employees or players when it comes to spreading goodwill. In fact, we're hosting a gala fundraiser on December 19th. And everyone is welcome."

"That sounds fun," Leo whispered so as not to interrupt. "You two going?"

They shrugged, but he could see how their eyes lit up at the idea of a black-tie event. They reminded him of his sister.

He sat back as Miranda finished her presentation. She seemed warm and friendly, not at all like the cool, collected executive he often saw on television.

"I thought she'd be scary," he whispered to Violet as Miranda left the room.

"She seems nice."

"I guess she can be herself on home turf, where nobody's got her tied to an angry bronco."

Violet shot him a puzzled look. Sitting this close to her, he noticed she had faint freckles across the bridge of her nose.

"On TV," he explained, after clearing his throat. The press frequently had fun at Miranda's expense. He wasn't sure why, exactly—just was grateful he wasn't her.

"I guess I'd better volunteer, too," Daisy-Mae said, as the sign-up sheet got to their table.

"Why's that?" Leo asked.

"We commute together." She pointed to Violet, then scrawled her name on the page. Then she sighed and scratched it out. "Except I'm pretty sure I'm getting fired."

"What? Why?" The panic in Violet's voice had Leo leaning forward as well.

Her friend winced. "I kind of told off the PR team."

Leo bit back a bark of laughter when heads turned to stare at him. "Nuvella?"

She nodded.

She probably had it coming.

A break was announced and Daisy-Mae grabbed her phone, muttering something about missed calls before she hurried from the room.

"She runs a bunch of businesses in Sweetheart Creek," Violet explained.

"And the two of you commute? From way out there?" He'd heard the team captain, Maverick Blades, talking about the small town, and Leo had looked it up. Tiny and a bit more than an hour's drive away. A commute like that could wear on a person, even just a few days a week.

"We wanted to have a little fun," Violet said.

"Commuting is fun?"

She giggled. "No. Our jobs. And we're... having fun."

"Ah."

"We're the Dragon Babes," she stated, seeming almost embarrassed.

"Yeah?"

That blush returned to her cheeks, but she threw her shoulders back as though bracing herself. "We're both single, so we're going to enjoy all that this position has to offer."

Curious, he asked, "And what's that?"

For a long moment, Violet didn't answer. Finally, she said, "Date for fun even if you know it won't go somewhere. Go out for drinks and live a little. Meet new people."

He thought about that. "You mean party?"

Her upper lip curled in distaste. Okay, so maybe closer to introvert than party girl.

"Live like someone left the gate open?" he suggested, thinking of the old rodeo saying.

She smiled and nodded.

"It sounds like you've been living pretty seriously until now?"

"A trail of broken hearts follows me," she replied lightly. He had a feeling she was being sarcastic, but could see how she might break hearts. She had a way of worming into a guy's soul. Sweet and kind, but with enough unexpected quips to keep you on your toes. He'd wondered more than once since meeting her what she was up to at that moment.

"It's time for a bit of fun," she announced. There was a set to her jaw as if she was fighting something and unwilling to back down.

She definitely wasn't looking for the same things he was. He was ready to settle down—once he figured out how to find Ms. Right, aka Christine Lagrée, and convince her he was the one for a lifelong partnership.

"Well, I'm glad you have a friend here—even though she might get fired," he said with a wink. He was pretty confident Miranda would never allow someone like Nuvella to influence the hiring choices for her company. "Having Daisy-Mae here with you will make it all the more fun." And safer.

CHAPTER 3

*L*eo had less than an hour before he had to be on the ice for the pregame warm-up, but his nerves were killing him. Tonight was the first professional league game of his career. He'd been tossed off of vicious bulls, trampled, squeezed, had muscles ripped and shredded, but the idea of entering the rink with eleven other men who were at the highest level of this sport and had way more experience than he did? That was more nerve-racking than any rodeo he'd ever been in.

He'd already paced through every restricted area of the arena, trying to wear off his jitters, his headphones delivering a soothing sound bath Coach Louis had sent him. Music had helped him in bull riding, but today it wasn't coming close to lessening his nerves. He needed a distraction that would keep him preoccupied until just before he had to suit up. Once he was skating, he knew he'd be too focused to fret about all the ways he could mess up and get himself benched for the rest of the season. Assuming he even made it onto the ice during tonight's game.

The team's coach, Louis Bellmore, in an attempt to be reassuring, had said that nobody expected much from such a late bloomer, especially being on the league's worst-ranked team. Then he had grinned and slapped Leo on the back, seemingly oblivious to the fact that he'd basically flushed his right winger's hopes and dreams down the toilet.

Leo's wireless headphones beeped, then cut out as he reached the chilly, long hallway to the locker rooms. He tugged them off his ears and gave them a shake. He'd charged the set last night. They should be good for another eight hours, and he only needed a few more minutes.

"I can't believe they had us go dutch!"

Leo looked up, then instinctively turned to move in the opposite direction of the furious voice floating down the hallway. He needed a distraction, not drama about one of the players as relayed by a girlfriend.

"And split down the middle? I don't think so!"

What were women doing down here, anyway? This area was restricted to athletes, and this corridor specifically the Dragons.

The familiar voice grew closer and louder, the woman's indignation drawing his curiosity. He slowed his steps to listen. Maybe drama could be a decent distraction.

"Has the man never heard of math? Or was that crappy double date just a way to financially support his beer habit?"

Another woman laughed in reply, and Leo stopped.

"And a kiss? I should have socked him one. I hate dating!"

"I think your expression was sufficient," the second woman said with a laugh. "He'll never slide in for a kiss like that again."

"I doubt that very much."

Leo looked over his shoulder to see Daisy-Mae and Violet striding toward him, the latter's entire body vibrating with outrage. Daisy-Mae spotted the headphones swinging in his grip, stopped short and smacked her forehead with a palm. "I forgot to get our earpiece thingies from the charger upstairs." She gave Leo a quick wave and turned to head back the way they'd come. "Meet you in the locker room, Vi."

"Okay."

Leo leaned against the green cinderblock wall and pretended to be adjusting his headphones as he waited for Violet to reach him. She looked good. Red dress, her straight black hair clipped into some sort of twisted bun, with curled strands framing her wide cheekbones. Her bangs were swept to the side and her eyeshadow was what his younger sister called smoky. Sara-Lynn had spent hours practicing the look, vowing she was moving off the smelly ranch and becoming a makeup artist for the stars as soon as she graduated from high school. She'd gone to cosmetology school, but had married a cowboy. She seemed happy on her husband's family ranch, though, doing makeup for brides on the weekends.

"Hey," Leo said, as Violet moved past him. She gave a jagged sigh, and he focused on her puckered brow and frown. She looked like she was trying to hold it together. He fell into step beside her before he even realized what he was doing. "You okay?"

"Disaster blind date," she said, voice cracking, eyes blinking furiously. She bit her bottom lip so hard he was afraid she was going to bruise it or make it bleed.

"Dragon Babes failure?"

"I'm not cut out for this." Her voice was weak and it sounded like she might be holding back tears. She stopped walking and faced him, indignant. "I don't want to be serious and responsible for the rest of my life. I want to have some fun." A tear drew a line through the dark charcoal under her right eye.

"Don't cry," Leo said, wincing.

His sisters used to spin on him, pummel him with their fists when he said that. Apparently, crying was their release.

His, apparently, was fighting to stay dominant over a livid animal weighing as much as a pickup truck.

Or had been. He wasn't so sure what it was now, but he knew it wasn't tear-related, and that he still wanted to rescue anyone with tears in their eyes.

Violet gave Leo an incredulous look. Don't cry? *Don't cry?*

Was she supposed to bottle it up like a dude and explode later?

Did he not understand how *bad* her blind double date had been? The men had lacked basic manners and had belched and picked their teeth at the table. They'd undressed Daisy-Mae with their eyes the whole time and then had split the bill four ways—after inviting them to the most expensive place in the city and ordering a ton of beer! Which neither she nor Daisy-Mae had consumed.

Violet figured she could darn well shed tears of frustration and anger if she wanted to.

She put her hands on her hips and squared her shoulders. "Does crying make you uncomfortable?"

"I mean," he amended quickly, his eyes darting to the side, "you can cry if you want to..."

"That's right. I *can* cry!" Her voice was higher than normal, her indignation blatant. She knew she should hush, but it felt good to let her rage and disappointment out for once. "Nobody can see me when I'm in my costume, so I can cry the entire game while waving at everyone and blowing kisses. Nobody'll ever know."

Leo caught her arm, stopping her when she started to march off. She kept her eyes on his chest, afraid to look into those kind eyes of his. She'd already noted they had slashes of green through the dark blue irises. He tentatively wiped a tear from her cheek, and her body stiffened with a held-in sob.

The date, which had been before everyone had to work the game tonight, had been such a disaster, and he was being so incredibly nice to her. This was how crushes deepened. And she really couldn't afford that for a never-gonna-happen man like Leo right now.

"But I'll know you're crying," he whispered. "And it'll throw me off my game."

Was he trying to break her heart?

She brushed his hand away. "Don't be like that."

"Like what? A nice guy?" The hurt in his voice surprised her.

"Yeah," she said, crossing her arms. "You don't have to act like a decent human being."

"Why not?" Eyes narrowed, he echoed her posture, squaring off with her.

"It makes me feel stupid." Her voice was wavering again and she willed herself not to cry.

"How on earth does me being a nice guy make you feel that way?"

"Because I should know better!" Violet sniffed.

"And when you're nice after I've acted stupidly, it makes me realize how idiotic this whole Dragon Babes thing is. Yet if it doesn't work, I'll be cursed forever and stuck in this new version of me, which I'm not crazy about because then I'll surely be alone forever. And when you're nice, even though I'm acting like a basket case, it gives me hope that…" She caught her breath, realizing she was veering off the rails in the middle of the hallway.

So much for hopes of friendship.

"It gives you hope that nice guys still exist? And you just have to wait it out until one finds you?"

She looked away.

"Well then, I can see how annoying I'm being right now. Sorry for that."

She blinked, unsure whether he was about to turn cutting and mean. She felt like she was part vulnerability, where her heart still hadn't repaired itself from its last break, and part scary warrior, protecting it from further hurt. And she wasn't certain how much damage someone like Leo could do when she felt like this.

Leo tipped his chin upward as though egging her to fight, as though he wanted to test her mettle. "How about you quit rolling around in the

41

pigpen of your crappy date, dust yourself off and move on?"

She gave a snort at his tough tone and planted her hands on her hips. "So I'm not allowed to be angry?"

"You can be angry. But quit finding ways to amplify your suffering and roll around in the pain like it's worth something."

"Amplify my suffering? Have you never been single and on a horrible blind date?" She glared at him. "You know what? You're a jerk!"

"Most messengers are."

She huffed, but was so peeved by his honest delivery that she no longer felt like crying. She should walk away. Never speak to him again.

But somehow his straight-up, awful truths felt like a much-needed reality check. Life was way too short to wallow in something she should be laughing about.

Violet sighed, unsure how to stop taking herself so seriously.

"Coach Louis said this to me once." Leo placed his palms together and paused for a second. "Mistakes happen. Pain is inevitable—well, my mom said that bit about pain. But Louis said suffering is optional. You tried, Violet. You failed. Now you know that guy isn't the one, so move on." He watched her cautiously, as if he didn't know if he should duck and cover or chalk his words up as a win.

"I know I should."

His shoulders relaxed and he nodded to a passing official, stepping against the wall to let the man pass. "Good."

Violet's indignation flared again. "But he tried to kiss me at the end of the date!"

"Of course he did. You're cute."

She felt a jolt of pleased surprise from his compliment, but pushed past it. "The date was an obvious disaster, though. I gave absolutely no signs that a kiss was going to happen. Ever." She studied Leo's face, waiting for him to explain what her date had been thinking.

He shrugged thoughtfully, as though trying to find a way to encapsulate his gender in a few brief words. "Men reach for opportunities."

"Ones that aren't even there?" She felt ready to rip something apart. Something big.

"Men fail up."

"They what?"

"When men fail..." He selected his words carefully. "Have you ever noticed that they rarely get punished or fired? They'll receive promotions or new jobs with a fancy title. It's like everyone's too embarrassed to do anything about the situation."

"That's not true." She hesitated, considering his claim. "Is it?"

"Well, not on a ranch. You screw up, you're toast. Sayonara, pal. But in corporate, high-up positions it can be. And so some guys keep reaching and ignore the facts, because it's not really a true failure. Something comes out of it."

"This guy's not corporate." She sighed, feeling defeated all over again. "But he made a mess of our date and was still there with his hand out for the promotion."

"Which was…the kiss?"

She nodded, remaining silent for a long moment as she thought it over, her anger fading. "I need to do that more. Reach for it. Fail upward."

"Or pick a better date. Ask me which guys on the team are nice, then go out with them."

Violet studied Leo, judging his sincerity. They didn't know each other well, but it was a sweet offer. Especially as her doubts had grown about her ability to live life wild and free as a flirtatious puck bunny. It just wasn't who she was.

The idea had been to overcome her shyness so she could *then* find Mr. Right. It was going to take so long to get to the place she wanted to be that she wasn't even sure she'd make it.

"Okay, but one bad blind date and you're toast."

* * *

Violet, sweaty and exhausted after dancing around the arena in her dragon outfit throughout the game, took a shower in her locker room, then went to meet Daisy-Mae in the parking lot. She didn't know what she'd been thinking when she'd suggested they go out and enjoy the city's night life after work. She just hoped that Daisy-Mae was as disillusioned as she was by their earlier date and would want to go straight home instead.

It had been fun being in the stands, getting the crowd excited, hugging the little Dragons fans and working with Daisy-Mae. But Violet was tired now. More than she'd expected. Maybe her inner introvert needed some downtime after pretending to be an extrovert for several hours.

She slowed as she passed the players' locker room, where lots of people came and went, clogging the hallway. A nearby group broke apart, clearing a path for her. With her bag slung over her shoulder and her employee pass clearly visible, she kept to the wall, smiling shyly at anyone who passed.

A man with the fresh scent of shampoo and soap fell into step beside her.

Leo.

Her heart gave a little thump even though she knew he wasn't likely to consider her as the solution to any loneliness problems. At least not as more than a new friend in a new town.

A friend who'd had a meltdown in front of him mere hours ago.

But how could her heart *not* thump? He was gorgeous wearing all black, from his cowboy hat to his suit and boots.

She gave him a smile, proud that she wasn't dying of shyness. Progress! Sure, she wanted to comment on how he'd managed to get on the ice for the season's first game—not a common feat for a rookie, from what she'd heard. But her brain refused to cooperate and create any sentences for her.

When she finally summoned the words, she noticed Leo was peering at her from under his cowboy hat. Her shyness reared up again, shooting a flare of heat through her and making her tongue too big for her mouth.

"You don't look like you were crying in your costume during the game."

"Um, no. Someone wise told me that wallowing's not really worth it," she said, gazing down at the floor, watching his black cowboy boots land in time with her canvas sneakers. If she looked up at his dark blue eyes, she knew she'd go mute.

"Good call."

"Dating still sucks," she stated.

"No, blind dates suck."

"You're an expert?" She didn't know where her teasing tone came from, but the way Leo's face lit up made her wish she could summon that confidence all the time.

"Not really."

"Love 'em and leave 'em?" she asked, curious about the dating life of a hunk like Leo. It was probably golden and amazing. No pain, all gain.

He held the door for her at the end of the hallway, and she gave him a flirtatious look that surprised her. Wow. There was something about this guy that made her shyness fade fast. Maybe because she knew he'd never choose her, and he was associated with her mascot-as-a-way-of-being-more-extroverted plan?

"I went on a blind date once," Leo admitted. "It sucked."

Violet bet a hockey hottie's awful date meant his partner wasn't a perfect ten, or that her good-night kisses were a bit too wet.

"Yours sucked, as well."

"Did it ever," she agreed.

"If you look at the math, we're two for two."

"Bad odds."

"Only for blind dates."

"And everything else so far, which means there's only one thing I can do."

"What's that?" he asked with interest, taking the concrete steps up to the next level with the ease of someone with killer quad muscles.

"Give up."

He gave a low whistle. "Already? Wow."

"I had this whole vision of how fun this Dragon Babes thing would be."

"Kind of like a rebound?"

She nodded vigorously.

"You just came out of something serious?"

She nodded again. She still couldn't believe things with Owen were just…over. She hadn't even had a chance. She'd had it all laid out in her head, but now he was starting his life with someone else.

How had she done it again? Gone and seen something that wasn't there, like she had with

Wyatt? Or was that blasted curse messing up her love life?

"Broke his heart, huh? How long were you together?"

"Kind of hard when he barely knew I existed."

"What?"

Realizing she'd misled Leo about the seriousness of her relationship with Owen, she corrected herself. "No, not... I *was* in something long-term. But that was before."

She felt that familiar stab of embarrassment whenever she referred to her wedding day. The hurt that cut deep into her soul when she thought about how she'd been dressed and beautiful at the altar, believing her whole life was about to begin.

And then seeing Wyatt's eyes fill with panic. The way he'd been unable to say "I do." The pleading look of forgiveness as he shook his head, turned and jogged out of the church. Okay, it had started as a jog. Ended as a sprint. Until he hit the doors. They weren't push doors. They pulled inward.

One day she'd laugh about that.

She stopped at the top of the arena stairs and closed her eyes, bringing herself back to the present. "I mean, Owen and I were... He probably wasn't even that interested, or didn't realize I was, because he just got married. But we were moving closer to dating." She opened her eyes again. "I sound crazy."

She needed a dating coach or something. Like that guy Will Smith played in *Hitch*. Did they exist in real life?

"I'm a little confused." Leo had stopped walking, too, and drew her aside so people could pass through the busy area. "You were in something longterm, but the guy didn't know you existed?"

She hid her face in her hands, then dropped them. She'd finally managed to talk to a hunky guy, but of course couldn't seem to make any sense. "I was crushing on Owen from afar. Except we were friends, so not really from afar. I thought he noticed me, but obviously not."

"I find that hard to believe. You're this lovable, angry panda bear—impossible to overlook."

A panda bear? Really? Ugh.

"Pandas are chubby."

"They're cute, and you do seem to wear a lot of black and white."

"Hmm." She still wasn't so sure about being called a panda bear, even though he'd called her lovable.

"Okay, so we've confirmed the man is blind. Then what happened?"

"He married his ex."

Leo hissed as if in pain. Yeah, he was going to be a good friend.

"And get this," Violet said, leaning in. "He now rakes in millions a year in major league baseball."

Leo let out a low whistle. "No way."

"Way."

"So you have a thing for jocks?"

She laughed. Jocks were hunky, as well as part mystery with all that confidence, swagger and strength. But she wasn't exactly the type jocks noticed, Owen being a case in point. "One jock. One."

Leo's face fell. "So you don't have a little something going on for me?"

She laughed again, this time embarrassed. She *did* have a thing for him, but it was a flirtatious and fun, teasing thing. She knew nothing would happen between them and somehow that freed her to laugh, when normally she'd be dead from mortification by now. It was nice.

She needed to be careful or she'd get a verified crush on him, even though he was obviously un-attainable.

"Is your laughter a yes or a no?"

She shook her head.

"Too bad. I'm kind of awesome." His joking came easily; his smile was charming.

"I'm too shy to make any of this romance stuff work out."

She waited for him to confirm her fault, already dreading the sense of failure it would surely bring.

"But you're not shy around me. I mean, a bit at first. But you warm up pretty fast."

"That's because you're different," she stated, still unsure what it was about him that allowed her to be so free. "Most guys kind of overlook me or, um, see past me, like I'm not really there."

"These jocks you adore do this? Maybe you need to find a different type. A nice guy like me."

She giggled, knowing he wasn't actually putting himself up for consideration.

"You are a nice guy."

"I know."

"And thank you for letting me rant at you earlier."

"Yeah, I'm not your usual breed of cocky, arrogant, overconfident dude. Been tossed off enough bulls to have a healthy dose of modesty."

"Wow. Modesty. Yeah, I see that in you. Especially right now. Wait, unless you're actually saying you lack confidence?"

"Ouch!" He grinned and took a few steps back in his cowboy boots. "Be nice to me, angry panda."

"Fine. This better? You're humble. Kind and not intimidating. I kind of feel like I understand you and vice versa. You're not this big, scary mystery brimming with testosterone."

"And that's good?" His expression suggested he wasn't sold on that conclusion being a positive one.

"You're a friend."

He considered the statement but didn't argue, and that filled her heart with an unexpected warmth.

* * *

"Weird, isn't it?"

"What is?" he asked.

"How I can pour my heart out to you with all these famous hockey players streaming past us."

Leo glanced at the restricted area's foot traffic. He'd spent enough time around well-known sports figures that it rarely fazed him any longer, but he could see how it might lock up the jaws and minds of a regular Joe—or a shy bear like Violet.

But he had to agree when he stopped to think about it—the way Violet opened up with him was a bit like they'd known each other a lot longer than they had.

"You hear about people just clicking. And we clicked. Like we knew each other from a past life or something."

"That's not a thing," she blurted, her voice filled with skepticism.

"Soul mates?"

She frowned at him as if the idea of their clicking scared her a little.

"What do you believe in, then?"

"Curses."

"Curses? What kind?"

"I'm joking."

"So how do you explain our insta-friendship if you don't believe in the mechanics behind insta-friends?" Leo asked, leaning against the closest wall. The coolness from the cinderblocks seeped through his jacket.

"Did I say we're friends?" She tossed him a haughty look that made him grin.

"You did, in fact."

"We have the same personality—quirks? Or whatever. So we connect."

"Okay, fine. We're friends who share personality… bits. And we both have experience with crushing on someone from afar."

"I think that's actually pretty common."

"But I'm crushing on Christine Lagrée."

"She sounds famil—wait. You mean *the* Christine Lagrée with, like, a million followers? That Christine Lagrée?"

"The donor organizer for the Special Olympics."

"Oh."

He gauged Violet's surprise as recognition dawned across her face. Christine was collected, professional, frequently in the spotlight, had started a few trends on social media, and had even been in a few home-and-lifestyle-makeover reality TV shows. She might not appear at first glance to be Leo's type, but she was like him in that she knew what she wanted and would take no prisoners in her efforts to get there. She would help him project the right image to gain the life he wanted. She was exactly what he needed.

"I think we'd work well together," he stated.

"Well, learn from me. Don't just sit there waiting for her to open her eyes."

Leo considered the suggestion, having already noted that Christine didn't seem to con-

JEAN ORAM

sider him much more than a backcountry
cowboy. "Okay."

Violet scratched her nose, eyeing him.
"Shouldn't you be out with the other players,
chest bumping and flirting with blondes?"

"Not my thing."

"So, what have you done to get her to notice
you?" she asked.

"Who? Christine?"

She nodded.

"I sent her flowers."

"What? Why?" Violet looked so shocked he
laughed. "Are you stalking her? Does she even
know you?"

"Thanks for the vote of confidence. I'm not
super experienced with wooing, but give me
some credit. We've hung out with mutual
friends and I sent the flowers to congratulate
her."

"Oh. Okay."

"I may not have had anything serious or long-
term, but I'm not a creep."

"Sorry. Wait. You've *never*…?"

"Never what?" Unfamiliar embarrassment
filled him at the thought of Violet judging him
and thinking he'd fallen short. He hadn't really
been in a place where he'd had time to pursue a

56

romantic life. Surely she understood it wasn't a failing on his part?

The few times he had dated, they'd rarely gone out a second time. Life moved too fast for the luxury of dating for fun. But now that he wasn't on the road quite as much as he had been with rodeo, he was ready to pursue something. Something that would move him forward professionally. A strong partnership like his parents had on the ranch.

"Never had anything serious?" Violet's voice had lowered, and she stepped closer as though afraid to spill his secret to the people trickling past them from the arena's restricted area. "How have you gotten this far in life?"

Okay, so he was nearing thirty. But she didn't need to use that tone, as if she thought there was something majorly wrong with him.

"There are so many good women out there eager to snap you up. You must have a fatal flaw, like I do." Her eyes were wide, as though she'd just revealed proof that he was from outer space or something.

"Violet..." He sighed.

"And here you are roaming the wilds of the NHL, unattached." She seemed incredibly amused. It was endearing in an annoying kind of way. "Something must be so very wrong with you."

He planted his hands on his hips and scowled at her. "You're not funny."

He was busy. She was shy. There was nothing wrong with either of them just because they weren't romantically attached at the hip with someone.

"Well, who am I to talk?" she mused in a tone that suggested she was ready to leave the conversation behind. "I'm older than you are and still single."

"Right." He cleared his throat. They'd delved into their vulnerable sides, not something he often did. "We're just waiting for the right person and the right time."

"It's hard to keep believing that, once you've passed a certain age and all your friends seem to have a million 'right person' options lining up for them," Violet muttered.

"Well, I've been busy," Leo said, feeling the need to defend himself.

She started laughing and, unable to resist, he joined in.

"Why are we laughing?" he finally asked.

She shrugged, renewing their laughter. When his sides began to hurt, he held up his hands in surrender. His ability to laugh at himself so openly and freely with Violet left him feeling slightly dazed.

"I know I'm a mess," he admitted.

"No, I am. There's something wrong with me."

"I'm unavailable. And always have been."

"Really?"

"Yeah, and now I seem to expect marriage to fall into my lap." He sighed. "How crazy am I?"

"Well, I'm cursed and defective."

"No you're not. You're just shy."

"You haven't been left at the altar!" Violet blurted.

He gaped at her. "What? No!"

Violet jilted? She was so sweet and kind. Pretty, too. What sort of monster would do that to her? No wonder she was so quiet and reserved. An experience like that would decimate a person.

She was silent, her breathing coming hard. She looked as though she was waiting for the floor to swallow her. When whatever bad thing she'd been expecting didn't happen, she said tentatively, "That's how crappy my luck's been. So the Dragon Babes… Trying something new and, um, hoping for different results…"

She looked defeated.

"I'm not giving up, though," she whispered,

that same determination he'd seen at the new-employee orientation peeking through.

"Something good will happen," Leo insisted, giving her arm a supportive squeeze. He waited until she finally dared to look up at him. "You'll find what you're looking for. Just know what you want. Then expect it to happen."

There was a flash of vulnerability in her eyes. It was quick, but he recognized it. That shadow before she brushed it away. The fear of being alone forever.

"I can help you," she blurted out. "With Christine. She's a woman. I'm a woman. I'll help you win her."

"And like I said earlier, I'll help you find someone decent to date from the team. We'll turn around those bad blind-dating stats."

Violet was a gem. One who'd been knocked down by life but still refused to call it quits. He'd find her someone good. Really good.

"Deal." She grinned and put out her hand for him to shake. Just as he reached for it, his phone rang. He froze for a split second. Who would be calling him? Ignoring the call, he shook Violet's warm hand, savoring the touch.

"You gonna get that?" she asked, gesturing toward the ringing sound.

"Nah." He was enjoying this moment with Violet. "Oh crap! Sorry." He fished his phone from his pocket and turned away to answer it. "Hey, sorry."

"I'm out by the doors."

"I'll meet you there in a few." Leo popped his phone back into his pocket. "Sorry, gotta run."

"Hot date?"

He shook his head, feeling sheepish. "No. Just an old friend."

"Who you used to date?"

"A bit."

"And now that you're going to be hockey famous she wants a piece of you?"

He laughed. "Maybe. Although she knew me when I was a rodeo star."

"The one who got away?"

"Our road schedules never lined up enough for us to get serious." They'd settled in as friends almost a year and a half ago.

"Well, you'd better go."

He nodded, reluctant to leave. He enjoyed spending time with Violet. More than he'd expected to.

The two of them moved through the doors that led to the public part of the arena, where the crowds were thicker, but not too bad this long after the game. A few people waited hopefully in case players came through, and someone asked him for an autograph. Leo signed a notebook and glanced over his shoulder to check on Violet. She'd slowed her steps, watching him over her shoulder as well.

He waved, then turned back, just before a woman in tight Wranglers threw herself into his arms, nearly knocking him over.

His ex.

She still had that same dancing, sparkling smile and that familiar way of wrapping herself around him like she belonged in his arms. It was awkward. Especially since he had a feeling Violet was still watching. And for some reason, that idea bothered him more than he figured it probably should.

CHAPTER 4

*D*uring Thanksgiving dinner—held a day later due to a hockey game—at Maverick Blade's old farmhouse just outside Sweetheart Creek, Leo had been happily seated beside Violet. The guys, Maverick, Dak and Dylan, had teased him, and he'd teased them right back. He'd pushed it a bit too far with Dylan, the team's injured center, though. At one point he'd sent his own chair crashing as he tried to escape a fake lunge, after ribbing Dylan about being an older-than-average player.

It had been a fun night. Really fun.

But dinner was over now, another home game tomorrow night. Time to turn in and get some rest.

He found he didn't want to return to his sad, empty apartment. The atmosphere around the table had made him miss his family back in Montana. He'd be visiting next month, for the party his parents were throwing for their anniversary—something they'd never celebrated before. But at the moment he wished that date was coming sooner.

He also didn't want to say goodbye to Violet. He'd barely seen her since she'd agreed to help him woo Christine, almost two months ago. He got it, though. Her friend Daisy-Mae was dating Maverick, by the look of things, so Violet was commuting on her own. She may have even given up on her Dragon Babes idea, seeing as she was likely now flying solo.

As he walked across Maverick's yard, the late-November twilight having already settled in around them, he heard an engine click and struggle to start. After a moment of silence, the engine struggled again, not starting.

He turned, looking over his shoulder. An old car was parked a ways down from his, along the edge of the driveway. The dome light shed weak light over Violet and her dark curtain of hair resting against the steering wheel. As Leo walked over, she lifted her head as though sensing his arrival, and let down her window which whined and crawled.

"Car problems?"

She nodded.

"Pop the hood."

She obeyed, calling, "It's the battery. Clint told me I needed a new one, but I put it off."

"Who's Clint?" She'd already found a man and got him situated in her life? She hadn't mentioned that at dinner. But the woman was determined, that was for certain. He was surprised at the stab of disappointment he felt at the idea that she might now be taken.

"The local mechanic."

He smiled, tapping her car door. "I'll grab my cables and we'll get you going again."

He jogged to his old Toyota, started it and then drove across the grass, stopping his car so it was nose-to-nose with Violet's.

He popped his trunk, found his cables and waved them in the air. "Never leave home without 'em."

Violet got out and stood in the stream of light from his headlights, obviously uncertain how to make herself helpful.

"There we are," he said, after connecting the two vehicles. "You can start it up."

JEAN ORAM

"Why do you drive such an old car?" she asked, not moving from his side.

"You expected a truck?"

"Yeah. You're a cowboy turned hockey player. I thought trucks would be part of your man card."

He laughed at how serious she sounded.

He'd sold his big truck when he'd started working toward his NHL goal. He'd needed the private coaching time the extra cash could buy him, in order to catch up with players who'd been on the ice since birth.

"Why do *you* drive such an old car?" he countered.

"Because I hate car shopping."

"That's a silly reason."

"It's scary and foreign. I don't understand cars, or what salespeople are saying. I'm so afraid of getting ripped off that I just keep driving this one."

Leo considered the problem. "What's your budget?"

"For a car?"

"Yeah. I'm going to have to take you shopping."

She laughed. "Um, you promised you'd find me a guy on the team and you haven't done that yet."

"You've been avoiding me!"

"Have not!" She gave a snort of disbelief.

"You promised you'd help me get somewhere with Christine."

"So we're both reneging."

"Well, that ends now."

"Okay." She leaned over him as he adjusted a cable clip that was slipping off, holding the flashlight he'd propped on the air filter's lid so he could see what he was doing. She smelled nice.

"How about Landon?" he suggested, referring to the team's goalie. "He seems decent."

"Crushing on Cassandra."

"Really? Cassandra McTavish?"

"Yeah."

"I heard she moved out here to be closer to her sister, Alexa. We grew up in the same town back in Montana." He looked over his shoulder and met Violet's dark, bright eyes in the glow of the flashlight. Her lashes were longer than he'd realized and her quiet beauty struck him. How had he never noticed that before? "How about Dylan?"

She rolled her eyes. Right. Dylan had flirt-fought with Jenny from the Blue Tumbleweed shop in town throughout dinner.

"Okay, how about...Dak? That guy working

on the team's charity efforts—he was here tonight. Great guy."

"Totally in love with Miranda."

"Miranda Fairchild?" The team's owner? Interesting.

Violet nodded.

"Well, I'll keep looking then."

"Send me plenty, because I'm cursed when it comes to love. Guys always leave me."

"Can't be true."

"Still single."

"Which is a crime, I tell you."

"Preach it, brother."

He chuckled and wiped his hands on a rag he kept tucked under his hood. "Okay. Go start your car."

Violet flashed a smile and slid into the driver's seat. She grinned when the engine came to life, and leaned out the window. "Thank you!"

Leo coiled up the cables, wanting to stretch out his time with Violet, but unsure how. He turned to stare when she turned off her car and got out.

"What are you doing?" he demanded.

She stopped moving. "Saying thank you?"

"Your car needs to run a bit to charge up the battery again."

"Oh." Her face flamed red in the stream from his headlights. She groaned and tipped back her head.

"It's smart to turn it off when you get out. It's a good habit. Otherwise your car could get stolen, right?"

She nodded, biting her bottom lip.

"Pop your hood and I'll boost you again. Unless, of course, you're just doing this as a weird way to flirt with me." He grinned as the color in her cheeks darkened.

"That's it. I'm buying a new car on Monday," she grumbled, reaching in to release the hood again.

Leo laughed. "Maybe we should go together. Because apparently my car is *old*."

As she retook the driver's seat, he saw something flicker in her eyes. That devilish playful side she sometimes let out, he suspected, but she remained disappointingly quiet.

She restarted the car and Leo released the cables, closing the hood. He pointed at her. "Now don't turn it off until you get home."

She nodded.

He came to the window, coiling the cables. "I'm going to follow you to make sure you don't stall again. You don't want to be stranded out in the country somewhere. Especially in the dark."

She eyed him for a beat, then batted her lashes and said, "Well, that's no fun. I was planning to turn it off at every stop sign between here and home to see if I could catch myself a cowboy."

He bit back a smile. "If I didn't know better I'd think you left your lights and radio on earlier so you'd find yourself in this very predicament." He tipped his cowboy hat meaningfully.

"Who said you're still a cowboy and that I'm trying to catch *you*?"

He glanced down at himself. He was wearing cowboy boots. Nice jeans. Button-down shirt. Cowboy hat. You couldn't take the cowboy out of the man. Not one who'd had to fight for the family ranch at age eighteen and had ridden bulls for a living.

It was true, though, sadly enough. She wasn't looking for a guy like him, and he wasn't looking for a gal like her.

He just shook his head and sighed, as if she'd broken his heart. Then returned to his car, making good on his promise to escort her home.

* * *

Leo had followed her all the way home, and as usual, Violet slowed her car as she came around the curve of her driveway. She was still in love with her house after living there for almost two years. It was an older two-story that had once been a bed-and-breakfast called Peach Blossom Hollow. She had kept the name and sign, nailing a Closed banner across where it used to say Vacancy. An ancient fixture positioned above the sign lit it up, welcoming her home.

Her driveway was lit by a yard light and the veranda lights showed off her peach-colored house with the black-and-white trim, giving it a pretty evening glow that felt almost magical.

Wild roses grew along the curving drive, highlighted by her headlights, and a few peach trees framed the house. They blossomed each spring, and by late summer, dropped peaches over the short picket fence that enclosed a small yard, carved out of the several-acre lot.

She loved everything about her little nest, and its warmth made her introverted side never want to leave it.

She parked in front of the house and got out to thank Leo, who'd followed her in.

"Are you going to be able to get it started in

the morning?" he asked through his open window.

She glanced at her car, unsure.

"Do you have a charger?"

She shook her head.

She wasn't far from town, less than a quarter of a mile, situated in a meadow between the town and the local swimming hole. She could easily call a tow truck if the car didn't start. And then after the holiday weekend she could get it in to see Clint.

But she might need a boost again after to-morrow night's game. Lately, Daisy-Mae had been commuting with Maverick more and more, due to her new full-time position in the team's head office. She hadn't been fired for telling off Nuvella; she'd been promoted to a desk job as well as still serving as Violet's handler at home games. And that meant Violet couldn't always rely on her for commuting to games, since she'd already be in the city.

Violet's car-fixing procrastination had finally caught up with her. She could ask Daisy-Mae, but was certain that would mean a change of plans for her friend. Even though tomorrow was Satur-day, she was fairly certain Daisy-Mae would be riding in with Maverick for the game. Those two had started dating as a publicity ruse, but things were looking pretty real to Violet these days and she didn't want to interfere. Even if it left her stuck here in Sweetheart Creek.

"I'll think of something," she told Leo.

"You could get a new battery tomorrow," he suggested.

"Everything in town's closed until Monday."

She needed a partner. This was one of those moments when it felt overwhelming to be an adult, to be alone. Too many problems of her own doing and not enough solutions.

Leo had gotten out of his car. "Raise the hood again." When she released the latch, he pulled out his phone, and snapped a photo of her battery. "In the morning we'll get you a new one in the city."

"We?"

"Well, you're stuck here unless you have a second vehicle." He looked around, spotted her Vespa parked near the side of the house under a light and frowned. "We have a home game to-morrow night, so you can't wait for Clint." Leo had his phone out again. "I'll catch a ride into the city with Dylan tonight, if he hasn't headed back already. You can take my car tomorrow."

Violet cringed. While she loved how Leo was stepping in to help, she also hated it. Not because he was rescuing her, but because he was going to ask someone for help who had teased him so relentlessly throughout dinner tonight. And sure, Leo, in several cases, had definitely started it. But still. There was some weird power struggle happening there. Or maybe it was simply a guy thing. Either way, it was weird and she didn't know whether to laugh along like everyone else or try to put a stop to it.

"It's fine. I'll tell Daisy-Mae she has to drive me."

"I'll pick up the battery in the morning." Leo continued as though she hadn't protested. "Then after the game we can drive out here in my car, replace your battery, and you'll be good to go for Sunday morning if you need to be anywhere."

"Leo!"

"What?"

"That's a ridiculous plan."

"Why? What's wrong with it?"

"First of all, how are you going to get a battery tomorrow morning with no car? Second, it's way too much driving—especially after tomorrow's game." They wouldn't get out here to swap out her battery—in the dark—until midnight, at the very least.

"First of all," he said, emulating her tone, "they

have these things in the city called ride sharing, taxis, buses, limos…"

She snorted. "You're going to take a limo to the auto parts store?"

He shrugged. "Why not?"

"You won't." She knew him. He wasn't flashy. He was a cowboy through and through. Conservative. Careful. Considerate. The man probably had at least ten grand stuffed under his mattress "just in case." Ten grand that would still be there after his death because he'd never spend it. And in the meantime, he'd drive that old Toyota. "A limo? Come on."

He frowned and crossed his arms, giving her a long look. "Wanna bet?"

"It's ridiculous."

"Maybe I'm ridiculous."

"That you are. And this, right here, is why we're friends, but will never be lovers," she said, laughing. "We're too different. I can get a boost tomorrow, then drive into the city to find a place to get this all fixed before the game." She dusted her hands together. "Look at that. Non-ridiculous problem solving."

"Maybe I enjoy being ridiculous."

"I don't believe you can do frivolous and

ridiculous. That's actually where you're like me—you don't have it in you."

"Really?"

She leaned forward. *"Really."*

"Be at my place tomorrow morning at seven."

"Seven? No way."

"Scared to see yourself proven wrong about my ridiculousness?"

"How will I get there so early? The guy who drives the tow truck would kill me if I woke him up at 4:00 or 5:00 a.m. for a non-emergency."

"I said seven."

"I need boosting and driving time."

"But you're taking my car and I'm going to—"

"No way. He was mean to you!"

"Who? Dylan?" Leo frowned as if she was talking crazy. But at one point, even with his foot in a cast, the athlete had lunged at Leo, sending him running. They'd laughed it off, but there'd been some posturing involving a lot of testosterone going on between the two of them. It was just... No.

"You don't have brothers, do you?" Leo asked.

She shook her head.

"That teasing was not mean. Trust me. Unrelenting, yes. But Dylan actually kind of accepts me."

She shook her head again, this time in disbelief. "Men are weird."

"So how do you plan to see me in the limo as I ride to the parts store if you don't take my car and won't call for a boost?"

"I'm coming to town tonight, and I'll stay in a hotel."

"You're too cheap to change out your car's battery, but you'll stay in a hotel just to see me in that limo?"

She giggled. The entire conversation was becoming ridiculous. "I'm selectively cheap. I like hotels and they're way more comfortable than dealing with car issues. Plus I've never ridden in a limo, so I'm curious."

"That settles it then. You have to come to the city with me tonight, because tomorrow we ride."

* * *

"I didn't realize the city would be so busy this weekend," Leo said apologetically.

"I guess a lot of people come to visit family, but don't actually want to stay with them for the holiday," Violet replied, rubbing one arm nervously as he unlocked his apartment door.

Leo felt he should drive her back to Sweetheart Creek, as their joking around had led her here—to San Antonio, where there wasn't a single available hotel room close to his place. Her staying in his guest room felt like it could be construed as an elaborate setup on his part.

"I promise there are clean sheets, fresh towels, and I'm tidy. If you want a lock on your door tonight, I can switch the lockable handle from the bathroom to your bedroom."

"That's not necessary." She remained in the doorway, watching him, after he swung the door open. "Unless you have some deep, dark secrets you want to tell me about?"

"I don't."

"You're nervous."

"Yeah." Strangely so.

She gave him a coy look, and his nerves gave another jump.

He couldn't seem to settle himself. They were friends. He was helping her out and tomorrow he'd be treating her to a limo ride. What was the big deal?

She was a woman.

In his space.

Overnight.

That didn't happen in his world.

But she was a friend. And she'd remain a

friend, which meant nothing was going to happen. Which meant he should chill out.

Violet's tone softened. "I don't have to stay if you're uncomfortable—"

"No, it's fine," he said quickly. "You're just very private and I don't want you to feel as though—"

"I'm private?"

"Very."

"I guess that's true." She swept through the doorway, moving with the grace of a queen. She slid the strap of her pink overnight bag from her shoulder and let it fall to the floor as she slipped off her shoes.

"You can leave them on."

She glanced back, her eyes dropping to his boots as though questioning why he wouldn't remove them.

Leo paused a beat. He knew it was a Japanese tradition to remove ones shoes. Was it Korean as well? He shrugged and balanced on his right foot while using both hands to wrangle a boot off the left. Switching legs, he hopped across the linoleum floor, working on the right boot. With them tossed aside, he followed her into the apartment, trying to see it from her point of view.

He realized with a glance that it was sorely lacking. Her place, from what he'd seen while she'd been packing her overnight bag, was homey and cute.

He bet she had real art and matching furniture. Meanwhile, the only things hanging on his walls were tacked-up workout and meal plans from the team's trainer and dietician, Athena. His furniture was an uninspired collection gathered mostly from front yards, under signs that said Free. In essence, everything important to him could be packed in his car and taken with him at a moment's notice, the rest left behind.

"You don't have much," she noted, poking her head into his living room.

"The habit of living lean is hard to break."

"Yeah?" She eyed him. "Is that why you're so stingy with yourself?"

He smoothed a hand down his pale green shirt. "I'm not stingy."

"Uh-huh." Her tone said she was unconvinced.

"I was on the road a lot with rodeo, sending money home. Since leaving the ranch I've never really stayed anywhere for a long period. Nowhere you'd really call home."

He was building toward buying one, but he wasn't sure where it would be, seeing as players could be traded to other teams with little notice.

Buying a home may have to wait until he was out of the NHL.

Violet was peering into the guest room, and he hurried ahead of her so he could turn on the lights, close the blinds and collect the hockey equipment spread out over the black futon. He shoved it all into bags lined up against the wall.

"Sorry it's not much."

"Impressive."

Leo took in the room again. He saw nothing about the architecture or decorating that could be considered impressive.

"It doesn't smell like gear." She waved her hand.

"I try not to stink." He began collecting the bags, then paused. "Would you prefer to use my room? I can sleep in here if you want."

"This is fine."

"The futon, it's, uh…" He dropped the bags and laid the futon flat, feeling self-conscious.

He had no idea how he'd gone from boosting her car after Thanksgiving dinner to having her as an overnight guest. It was already past midnight and tomorrow was a game day. He was normally so rigid about his diet, training and sleep patterns. But tonight he felt like it was all unreal, his energy wild and restless.

Maybe it was just nerves, which was weird because this was Violet. But currently, he was even more nervous than she seemed to be.

"Are you hungry? Thirsty?" He wished he could cook more than the basics. Casually whip up something that would dazzle her.

"I'm good. Carol overfed me."

Maverick's mom had indeed overfed them all. It had been wonderful. She'd taken over Maverick's kitchen and had been well prepared to feed a bunch of young athletes.

"How about a glass of wine? No, I don't have wine." He was trying to play host and failing. "No drinking during the season. Or at least limit it. I have herbal tea?" He winced. If anyone asked for his man card right now he wouldn't argue, just hand it over.

"That would be nice, thank you."

She looked pleased with the offer and they moved from the guest room. He stacked the hockey bags in the hallway closet and continued the tour, which took approximately another thirty seconds. He pointed out the bathroom, his room—she laughed, spotting a loud-patterned Hawaiian shirt he'd bought for a party—the living room again, and then the kitchen.

"Are you a minimalist?" she asked when he

pulled out two cups from a cupboard, revealing his sparse set of dishes. "Other than your belt buckle collection."

She was smirking at him and he found he was really beginning to adore the way she teased him.

He'd been wondering how long it would take her to tease him about the rows of shiny belt buckles on display on his dresser. He'd won them at various rodeos over the years and they were his prized possessions. Each one represented courage and battle—battles he'd won.

"Nah, I just live like a minimalist." He glanced around. "Maybe that makes me an accidental one?"

"You're not tempted to blow your big pay-checks on material possessions?"

"Oh, I am," he said with a laugh. He had a long list of dream items. "I just don't want to lose it all before I begin, you know? Plus, Miranda told me this story about her granddaddy and how his NHL days ended abruptly. It's basically my biggest fear at the moment. That it could all end and I'd be caught out—financially."

"What happened?"

"An injury early in his career, right after he'd overspent. Financially, it broke him."

"That's horrible." Violet filled the kettle from the tap. "Did you do well in rodeo?"

He hitched up his belt with pride. The buckle on it was large and shiny, the equivalent of an NHL championship ring.

"What?" Violet was frowning at him as if he'd offered to take off his pants or something.

"My rodeo buckle…"

"It's big?"

He chuckled softly. "You didn't grow up around here, did you? It's an award. Like a trophy you wear." Feeling humbled, he turned to the counter and pulled down boxes of tea. "What kind do you want?"

She reached for the ginger peach. "I know it's an award. I was making sure you hang on to your modesty badge."

He snorted and shook his head, taking the box of tea from her. "Hot or cold? I have ice, I think."

"Hot."

"Again, where did you grow up? Texans like their tea iced."

"I'm Texan."

"I don't hear a twang."

"Well, I grew up in Chicago, then came out here when I was in high school. I moved to Sweetheart Creek a few years ago, *y'all*."

The electric kettle clicked off a minute later, and he poured water into their cups, then led the way into the living room, relieved that he at least had a comfortable couch and coffee table.

"You know…" Violet began, after a moment of blowing the steam from her cup. "For a jock you really aren't very smooth with women, are you? But you're serious about me helping you with Christine?"

* * *

As they settled on the couch with their tea, Violet could see Leo starting to relax. She loved how nervous he was about her ending up at his place for the night. His efforts to do right and help her endeared him to her all the more.

"So what do you need with Christine? Has she still not noticed you?"

"Not as someone other than a friend who keeps popping up at the same parties and fundraisers. And you're still searching for Mr. Right?"

"I'm still holding you to helping me find him."

He turned his cup in his hands so the handle was away from him, then took a sip.

She took a sip of hers, then tapped the cup. "This is good."

"I like peach."

"Me, too. Did you know my place used to be a B & B called Peach Blossom Hollow?"

"I saw the sign. It's a nice spot." He looked around his apartment with an expression of longing she understood. He wasn't happy here. It was a holding place, nothing more.

How long could a man live like that?

Maybe that was why he was so eager to find someone, even someone who wasn't quite the right fit.

She shifted, getting more comfy. "So, Christine Lagrée? You know what she likes and wants?"

"Jewelry, chocolate, flowers?"

"Some women enjoy traditional gifts. Does Christine?"

"I'm not sure."

"Well, most people like to know that they've been thought about…"

"Do you like gifts?"

"The right gift, yes. But if Christine didn't really warm up to your flowers, she might want something different. You need to pay attention to what she likes and responds to if you're hoping to woo her. Maybe she'd like you to plan an outing for the two of you. You know, show her some attention. Or maybe she likes compliments."

"Compliments? She's not superficial."

"It isn't superficial to feel good if someone compliments you."

"I guess not. It just seems, I don't know... Fake? Disingenuous to start complimenting her, like a pat to her ego, especially when she works hard for an organization like the Special Olympics."

"You think she'd be above compliments? Even genuine ones?"

"Yeah."

"Hmm." They sipped their tea. "Your shirt looks nice. It brings out the color of your eyes." All night she'd kept getting caught by how his dark blue eyes seemed mountain-lake-blue due to the green in his shirt. "I'm glad we're having this cup of tea and getting to know each other more."

"Thanks. Me, too." He smiled, one of those warm, sweet ones where she knew he was feeling good. Interesting. Kind words filled his cup in a way Violet hadn't expected. Maybe because he was still such a self-reliant cowboy it could easily seem that he might be above needing to hear nice things about himself.

Which was silly because, man or woman, didn't everyone like that?

Even big-hearted women like Christine.

Violet laughed. "Those were examples of nice words. Compliments."

"Oh." His shoulders dropped.

She laughed again, charmed by his reaction, then reached over and gave his arm a quick squeeze. "But they were genuine."

In fact, she was a bit in awe that her jaw hadn't locked up, complimenting him so truthfully, so genuinely. Was it the fact they were solidly in the friend zone that she could be at ease around him even though he was such a tremendous hottie?

"They were nice. Thanks."

"You're welcome."

"I should compliment people more. And I get your point about Christine."

"Cool. So you can also try doing things for her."

"Like fixing a car?" Leo gave Violet a pointed look.

"Yeah, actually."

"Okay, well, Christine has a new car…"

"But other things. Like if she's at an event and carrying her coat everywhere, you could offer to take it to the coat check, or hold it for her."

88

"But that's so small."

"It doesn't mean it doesn't matter."

"So those men at the malls holding purses and coats are actually wooing their ladies? They're not just whipped by their wives?"

"Well, maybe sometimes. Just a little."

Leo laughed when she grinned. "Okay, more. This is good stuff." He lifted his cup and looked around as though he'd misplaced something. "Should I be writing it down?"

"I'm not going anywhere. Remember, I'm your Yoda."

"Okay, Yoda. Hit me up with more."

"Umm..." Her cheeks heated as she thought of one other tip she could give him.

Leo noticed. "What?"

"Kisses, holding hands, touching." She couldn't look at him.

When she finally dared look up, his cheeks were pink, making her feel better about her own discomfort.

"So what do you think Christine would en-joy?" Violet asked. "Compliments?"

"Not sure."

"Well, whatever she responds to, I think you can stand out just by being yourself."

"She doesn't want a cowboy."

"Why's that?"

"She's sophisticated. I need to be a bit more urbane."

"But cowboys are charming and solid folk. Loyal and reliable, typically." Her ex-fiancé, a cowboy, had kind of failed on a few of those points, though. "I bet she just needs to hear you speak your heart and she'll be won over for life."

Leo's lips curled. "I'm not sure about that."

"Whatever you do, don't change."

"I won't. But I need to highlight the things I *can* offer. Things she might want."

The whole wooing Christine thing was starting to stink. Leo was a great guy and to see him chasing someone who might not recognize that…well, what a waste.

"What?"

Violet made sure she smoothed her expression to hide her thoughts. "Nothing."

"You think this is dumb."

"*You* think *Dragon Babes* is dumb."

He opened his mouth, then shut it again.

"So we both want to change a tiny bit to attract someone who brings out the better, more interesting side of ourselves," she said, not looking his way.

"A partnership that takes us where we want to go."

"Makes us better people. And I want love, too."

They were quiet for a long moment.

"Does love really matter?" he asked.

"What do you mean?"

"Is it even real? Or is it a trick we tell our-selves? Some old instinct to keep us in the pack and increase our survival?"

"Wow. You're jaded."

"No, I don't think so."

Violet sat up straighter. "Wait. Have you never fallen in love?"

"I don't fall in love, no."

"Have you ever had a chance to?" She thought of the woman he'd dated on the rodeo circuit. The one who'd draped herself over him at the rink when Violet had been pretending to walk away, but had secretly been watching over her shoulder.

"Sure. I guess. Maybe. I don't know."

"How do you not know? It's *love*."

"I love my parents and family and would do anything for them. But romantic love is different."

"A bit."

They were silent with their own thoughts

again.

"How would you describe falling in love?" Leo finally asked.

Violet pondered that for a long moment. "Falling in love is like taking a step off a cliff and trusting that the air will catch you. That you're not just throwing yourself onto the rocks below, where you'll get broken. It's the most difficult thing, the biggest act of trust."

They sat in thoughtful silence, Leo reaching across the open space on the couch, resting his hand there, palm-up, as if waiting for her to do something. She stared at the callused skin, the hand that worked so hard for himself, for his family. She glanced up at his face, then gently laid her hand in his.

Friends.

Leo lifted their hands, then set them down with a squeeze before releasing her. "Well, it's a good thing I'm not going to do any of that."

"Do what?"

"I'm not going to fall for Christine. I'm not going to break her heart and she's not going to break mine."

"How can you guarantee that?"

"Because I'm not the kind of man who falls in love."

CHAPTER 5

*V*iolet heard Leo in the kitchen, starting breakfast, as she climbed off the futon in his guest room. They'd stayed up late—way too late considering that tonight was a game night—chatting on the couch for hours. They'd bared their souls, and it felt like he'd told her stuff he'd never told anyone else. He'd poured out the whole story, in her opinion a heartbreaking one, of how he'd joined the pro rodeo circuit to save the family ranch. He'd given up scholarships and his dream of going to college, staying in the dangerous sport to ensure his three siblings could grow up on the same land he had.

Her growing crush on him certainly wasn't going anywhere now.

And that spelled trouble, didn't it? He was looking for Business Barbie to be his bride, and Violet was looking for a man who wanted to put down roots.

It was her friend Hannah's birthday, and she gave her a quick call. Of course Hannah Murphy, back in Sweetheart Creek, had somehow learned where Violet had spent the night, and between telling her son to stop chasing the dog, had drilled her with a hundred and one questions.

Just friends. Just friends. Just friends.

Was there a worse expression in the English language?

In return Violet teased her friend, saying that the For Sale sign next door to her was soon going to turn to Sold, and that Mr. Dreamy Pants would be moving in to sweep her off her feet. Her divorced friend had choked with laughter and referenced something about Florida freezing over before that ever happened.

Violet ended the call, sighing loudly as she headed to the bathroom. Love. It was so hard to find.

The bathroom was steamy and warm from Leo's shower, and she longed to soak in the tub and let her problems wash away.

"Hungry?" Leo called, coming down the hallway to look for her.

She opened the bathroom door.

He had a frying pan in hand. "Breakfast is almost ready..." His voice faded as he took her in.

"Ugh, don't look at me." She covered her face. Her eyes always looked especially puffy right after she woke up.

"You're a cute, grumpy little panda first thing in the morning." He was using an adorable, annoying cutesy voice and she rolled her eyes. And he was sticking with the panda bear thing, too, but somehow she didn't mind. It made her feel special that he'd given her a nickname, even though it wouldn't have been her first choice. "No makeup on your sleepy face. And look at your perfect black hair. Cutie-patootie."

"You're going to die. You know that, right?"

"Breakfast?" He held up the pan of slimy, halfcooked eggs.

She peered at his offerings and grimaced. "Are you going to cook those some more?"

"Of course. I just didn't want them to burn."

"Well, this far from the stove I don't think that's likely." She went back into the bathroom. What was it about dealing with that man? It felt like she was flirting, then snarky all in one breath.

95

"Ready in two minutes!"

She washed her face and changed out of her PJs. She heard a blender go on in the kitchen and meandered that way, secretly loving that he'd made them breakfast.

Buttered toast, eggs and fruit were set out, and she took a spot across from where she assumed he'd be sitting.

"Game day." He lifted the blender, which held something green and gross looking. "I love saying that. Do you have a special game day breakfast?"

She gave a shake of her head, watching him pour the contents into a tall glass. "Does Athena make you drink those?"

"Yup." He swallowed half of it. "Best if you down it fast," he said, his voice choked.

"Worth it?" she asked, when he set down the empty glass, then turned to chug water.

"I love being part of a team. I can lean on these guys, you know?"

"You couldn't in rodeo?"

"Oh, yeah. Those guys will always be anywhere you need them in a heartbeat."

"Did they tease as much in rodeo?" she asked, thinking of Dylan O'Neill and the weird vendetta thing between him and Leo.

"Sure. Rodeo's family. So's hockey. But it's different."

"Which do you love most, or is it too early to tell?"

"I love 'em both, but I have a feeling I might come to love hockey even more." He winked at Violet and she felt the heat hit her hard. She reminded herself that him coming to love hockey more would have nothing to do with her involvement in the sport. It was about the game, plain and simple.

"What time do you have to be at the rink?" she asked, trying to focus on eating.

"We have lots of time to go to the parts store. The limo will be here in forty-five minutes. I hope that's okay?"

She nodded and tipped her head down, busying herself with spreading jam on her toast.

"How is it?" he asked after a few minutes.

"Good." Her eyes darted upward, raked over his broad shoulders, then dropped back to the plate. Man, he was hot. And this moment felt so… weighted. Domestic.

Something she wanted and could get used to.

She'd known she was lonely, but this…this was really stirring it up. Normally, she would be tired out after spending so much time with someone she didn't know very well, but Leo was different. She felt like she could spend eons with him and never need her own quiet space to think and recharge.

"How many stars?"

"Oh. Um. The meal? Four and a half."

"Nuts. I was hoping for a perfect five."

"I prefer rye toast."

"Really?"

She shook her head. "I actually like cinnamon-raisin best."

"Hey, I made coffee and tea. Want some?"

"There's both?"

"Yeah. I didn't know what you preferred in the morning."

She got up and poured herself coffee, then sat again. Deliberately swallowing her shyness, she teased, "Look at you, working those wooing tricks. Be careful or you'll have me stalking you, lurking around and expecting all this special treatment."

He laughed. "Get used to it. You're my practice girlfriend."

She coughed in surprise. "Your what?"

"You know, to practice all those things you taught me last night. Compliments, gifts, doing nice things for you and such."

Right. She'd told him to do that.

With *Christine*.

He spoke his next words carefully. "We're still helping each other, right?"

Her shoulders drooped. She wasn't sure she could handle a man like Leo turning all his charm on her without feeling it was genuine and truly meant for her. She already had enough issues, seeing what wasn't there between her and nice guys, without having a hottie like him pouring it on thick.

"We don't have to," he said quickly.

"No. No. It's fine." Violet rested her elbows on the tabletop, her chin on a fist. She needed to figure this out. She wanted to help Leo. And honestly, the sooner she got him married off, the sooner she could outgrow this somewhat inappropriate crush on her friend and head off to meet Mr. Right. "I'm just tired."

"Oh man, me, too. I hope I don't crash during tonight's game. I haven't stayed up talking like that in...well, ever." He pushed a hand through his hair and his eyes met hers. "There's something about you where I pour it all out, you know? You're safe."

"Thanks." She felt heat spreading across her cheeks and her jaw locking up on her.

"And it was nice having company. If you ever want to stay here instead of traveling home after a game, just say the word."

She shook her head.

"No, the offer's genuine."

She gave him a sly smile, forcing back her shyness. "I couldn't, because I'd soon be cramping your style."

He laughed, lifting his glass of water to her coffee cup in a toast. "We can only hope."

* * *

Violet couldn't believe Leo had actually rented a limousine to take them to the parts store. This man who drove a beater like her, because he couldn't bear to pay for something new, had hired a limo. When his own car was right there in the parking lot, ready to go. She couldn't wrap her mind around it. Leo was unlike any man she'd ever met. He was serious, focused and driven. But he was also playful and fun. He was up for an adventure, but also balancing life and responsibility in a way that looked easy. It looked like something she wanted.

"Drink?" he asked, opening a side panel near the limousine's rear seat. She'd overlooked it, assuming it contained a fire extinguisher or fuses. But inside was a minibar.

"No way! That's a fridge?" Violet slid forward on the soft leather, the lack of restraint causing her to hesitate for a second. Why didn't people have to wear seat belts in a limo?

On the lookout for other secrets and surprises, she glanced around the interior, feeling like a kid again. She loved stories where the characters discovered hidden passageways or compartments, and she'd spent hours on her backyard swing imagining and willing her home to reveal secret passages to her. A stairway, maybe a half door hidden in paneling, a room revealed only if you pulled the right book from the bookshelf. Even a safe tucked behind a portrait would have been satisfying.

"I want this to be my next car!" she squealed when she pressed an indentation in the armrest and a lid popped up, revealing stereo controls. She touched a few buttons and soft music came through the speakers.

Leo laughed and held out a mini bottle of champagne as the limo glided down the city streets. "It's game day, so I can't drink, but you can."

"Leo! It's nine in the morning."

He shrugged. "Limo life."

She shook her head, unable to come to grips with the thought that champagne and limos were the norm for some. "It's game day for me, too."

"Did they give you a diet plan? Athena's been brutal with us, like she thinks what we eat can bring us together as a team and earn us some wins."

"Mascots don't have to perform at quite the same level. No fancy dietary plan for me."

Leo offered her an iced tea, which she accepted. She leaned back in the seat with a happy sigh, the cold bottle clutched in her grip. "I could get used to this."

"Me, too."

"Then why don't you? You have the means."

He shrugged.

After last night's heart-to-heart, she understood that he was like her, responsible and sometimes too serious. They'd both been raised that way—her by a strict Korean mother, him by a strict cowboy father. But she'd learned last night that he'd taken his sense of responsibility to the extreme with pouring his pro rodeo income straight into the family ranch rather than living high off the hog.

She gripped the cap on the iced tea before realizing she didn't know what it cost. In a limo a drink like this could easily run them double digits, couldn't it? She put it back in the fridge.

"What are you doing?"

She waved away his questioning look.

"You're not thirsty?"

"I'm good."

"Is this your first time in a limo?" he asked.

She nodded.

"You didn't ride in one to your—"

Wedding.

It was sweet that he caught himself midsentence.

"To my wedding? No. And I didn't ride in one to my prom, either. Did you?"

"Nope."

Violet noticed a glimmer of sadness in his eyes, and murmured, "There's so much I still don't know about you."

"Let's play Twenty Questions."

She smiled and snuggled deeper into the warm leather. She was familiar with the old game, and was pretty good at winning. "You're going first? What do you have in mind? Animal, vegetable or mineral?"

"No, not that version."

Her muscles tensed. At the girls-only engagement party they'd thrown for her friend Jackie Moorhouse, they'd played a version of this game. It was like a dirty adaptation of Truth or Dare, just no dares. And all questions about experiences with men. Her friends had hooted with laughter, each one comfortable being an open book, while she'd wanted to melt into the floor.

"If we're going to hang out, you need to relax and trust me." Leo's tone was amused and he gave her knee a quick squeeze.

"I trust you," she squeaked.

"You totally do not."

"I'm trying."

He studied her for a moment. "Fair enough. But you hardly ever tell me stories about you. You're very private."

"It's something I'm working on."

"Twenty Questions is a fast way to get to know you."

"Um…" She wasn't so sure about this.

"Trust me!"

She unclenched her fists from where they were bunched in her lap, and exhaled slowly. Violet couldn't believe she was agreeing to this. It was going to be humiliating and embarrassing just asking questions, let alone hearing the answers or giving them.

"Your first job?" he asked.

Her mind went blank and her cheeks went hot. She was *not* going to talk about *jobs*. She peered out the window, wondering how close they were to the store. Surely it wasn't that far from Leo's apartment.

"In high school? Babysitting?" he prompted.

She wanted to die. Just keel over, maybe be resuscitated. Maybe not.

Wait. She glanced at Leo, taking in his meaning.

"Do you mean like…work?"

"Yeah." He was watching her, head tilted, mouth quirked in a curious smile.

Now she could die. He didn't mean something sexual like hand jobs or…other kinds of jobs. What was it about this man that sent her mind down all sorts of crazy avenues?

Answers flew from her mouth, one on top of another. "Dog-sitter, paper route, tutoring, life-guard, more tutoring."

"Lifeguard? That's cool. In Sweetheart Creek? No. You grew up somewhere else, right?"

She nodded. "And what about you?"

"The ranch. But it wasn't paid work. Does that count?"

"Yes. But question one, subsection b is what was your first *paying* job?"

He paused for a second, a grin spreading across his face. "Pulling cars out of the parking lot at an outdoor concert after a big rainfall. The lot was just pasture, and it turned into this massive mud pit. All these cars kept getting stuck, and the more they spun their tires the worse it got. So I drove over there with my dad's 4x4 and started towing people out of the mud for ten bucks."

"How old were you?"

"Fourteen. I made over a hundred dollars."

"Fourteen! That couldn't have been legal."

He shrugged, rewarding her with a casual smile that made her stomach do funny things.

She shook her head. "Living in the country is very different from the city. The other day I saw this kid driving a big green truck. Whenever he had to shift gears, he would literally disappear under the dashboard. I've never been so afraid for my life as I was while sharing the road with him." When Leo failed to look perturbed, she added, "He was oncoming traffic. The driver literally vanished!"

Leo laughed, and she smiled, realizing that maybe she could tell funny stories about herself, and Twenty Questions could, in fact, be harmless fun. Usually she felt as though she wasn't interesting enough, and that people were always thinking she was weird or boring. But not Leo. He almost made her feel as though she wasn't introverted and self-conscious, but an interesting person he genuinely wanted to get to know better.

"Speed round," he announced. "Most random class you've ever taken?"

"Random?"

"Odd? Unexpected? Your choice. Surprise me."

"Cake decorating with a bunch of gals from town."

"Not weird. Handy."

"I'm not baking you a cake."

"Fine." He gave a dramatic sigh. "It's not on Athena's diet plan, anyway."

"How about you? Most useless class? Oddest? Maybe an unusual niche class?"

"How to ride an angry bull and not die."

She raised her hands in surrender. "You win."

They sat sideways on the bench seat, knees touching, watching each other as the limo purred toward their destination.

"Strangest skill you have. No, best skill."

"I'm good at math." She smirked, figuring that

he would assume she was telling the truth due to her Northeastern Asian heritage.

He narrowed his eyes. "You lie."

She giggled. "True. I'm average."

"Did I not mention in the rules that lying isn't allowed?"

She batted her lashes. "There are rules?"

"Are you flirting, Vi?" He leaned close, his warmth reaching her through the fabric of their clothes. She felt the terrifying heat, but fought it. Fought it hard. He was just a friend. She could totally handle this.

"You should be so lucky," she breathed, dropping her gaze to his lips.

He gave a low chuckle that tightened a cord inside her. She leaned forward, aiming for a mysterious, seductive tone as she said, "My odd skill is tango dancing."

His mouth was close to hers. "I said no lying."

"No lie."

He was silent for a long beat. "Teach me."

She laughed, leaning back in the seat. He was so earnest, so genuine. "A cowboy learning the tango?"

"I can do more than just ride around on animals."

"Fair enough."

"This is a deep one. Are you ready for it?" He leaned close again, and she felt as though the moment was a tipping point, that if she leaned forward herself they might kiss. Which was ridiculous. He'd reminded her only an hour ago that they were friends helping each other.

He was a nice guy. Definitely willing to help her. The last thing he needed was to have her swooning over him and making things awkward.

"Do you still believe in love after all you've been through?" His eyes were kind, his long lashes glorious. A man like him, moments like this...they made Violet believe the world was a good place, where women like her found lasting love.

She took her time, weighing the question as well as her response. She knew it was overly optimistic and possibly naive for her to still believe in love, and to relish that inkling of hope that flared up from time to time. Finding lasting love was still such a long shot. But if she could overcome her obstacles and get to where her life clicked into place, she felt she could have the things she wanted, such as family and a deep happiness.

"I believe in change," she said.

"That wasn't the question."

"But that's the answer."

"How so?"

"To believe in love, I have to believe in change. I have to believe that I can become someone who deserves it."

The muscles around his mouth tightened. "You *do* deserve love. No changes required."

"I will always be me," she said carefully. "But I can improve upon the parts that prevent me from having what I want."

He massaged his right knee as though it ached, his thumb digging into muscle.

"It's not that different from what you're trying to do," she pointed out.

He inhaled slowly, and the hard lines of his jaw, the tightness of his shoulders began to relax. "Fine. Fair point."

He met her eyes, but she couldn't sort out what he was thinking.

"So you believe?" he asked.

"Yes."

But what about him? He'd said he didn't fall in love. As if it was something he could prevent with sheer willpower.

"Leo?" She hesitated, summoning her nerve. "Do *you* believe in love?"

* * *

"It looks like we're here," Leo said, sliding forward in his seat, oddly relieved that the timing of their arrival prevented him from having to answer Violet's question. He wanted to believe in love. It felt like something he should want to believe in and have.

But so far love hadn't even thought of sneaking up in his rearview mirror, let alone sit on him with its two-ton weight. Why should he be so bold as to think it might happen to him? He didn't know *how* to fall in love.

He hopped out of the limo before the driver could come around, and reached inside for Violet's hand. She didn't budge for a few beats, and he thought she was going to refuse to leave her seat until he provided an answer.

"Well? *Do* you?" she asked pointedly, as though she understood just how deeply her question was stirring him up.

He tapped the face of his watch and shifted. "It's game night. We've got to keep moving."

"You're afraid of love!" she exclaimed with wonder, scooting out of the car, ignoring his offered hand. She was shorter than him by more than half a foot, but at the moment she somehow seemed taller.

"I'm not afraid."

"So you believe?"

"I didn't say that."

"Then what are you saying?"

He shifted onto his heels, unable to find words to describe that slightly desperate feeling of loss whenever he thought of his colleagues and their marriages.

"Okay." She placed her palms together, like she was going to pray. "Do you love your family?"

"Of course!"

"So you believe in love."

"That's not... That's not the same. It's different from what you're asking." He knew she was asking about that deep romantic love she was seeking.

"How is it different?"

"You're a real pest."

"I know." She nodded, her long black lashes fluttering as she blinked at him, unflappable in her dedicated persistence.

"Familial love is... You make sacrifices for family that go beyond obligation or duty. It's different from the love I would share with my wife." He wanted a family someday, and he assumed that would come with a whole lot of it. So why couldn't he just say that to Violet?

"Okay, and what's romantic love to you?"

"We're strangers who pass each other in the dead of the night. Unseen, unnoticed." Forgotten.

"But one day you might get noticed? By love?"

He guided her toward the store's entrance. "I'm regretting how comfortable you've gotten with talking to me."

"I know." She gave him a sunny smile, but refused to step into the store despite him holding the door for her and making an exaggerated sweeping motion with his arm.

"So you want love, but think you can't have it?" she asked.

Unrelenting. That was his current word to describe Violet.

"What year is your car again?"

She wouldn't budge.

He sighed. "Fine."

She gave a small bounce in place, aware that she'd won. She was adorable.

"I'd love to be married. Have a family. The whole happy package."

"I knew it!"

"But not yet," he warned, following her toward the shelves of batteries lined up on the north wall of the store. "I need to have a house that's paid for, and my retirement settled. I need to be done with hockey so I have time. So I can be attentive."

"You can be attentive during hockey."

He snorted.

"So basically you're going to be one of those eighty-year-old men marrying a woman in her twenties. I never quite pegged you as the type."

"Ew. No." He should have kept his mouth shut.

He was reading the labels on the wall to find the correct battery, but she stepped in front of him. "What's this that we're doing right now?" she asked.

"Me trying to get your car running."

"No, in the rules for wooing women."

"Quality pestering-me time. Move." He gently pushed her aside and reached for the battery she needed.

She pressed her way in front of him again, and he sighed, straightening.

"We're spending time together," she insisted. "And you've been attentive. This is like marriage. If we were married, this would be us enjoying domestic moments and a morning together. Breakfast, running errands…"

He knew he shouldn't imagine it—what it would be like to be married to Violet. How easy and fun it would be. That smooth, comfortable feeling of having a friend you loved in your house in the morning. Sharing moments, making memories out of the small things in life.

And there was that brief moment in the limo when he'd thought they were going to kiss...

"You have to have your affairs settled before you bring children into the world," he grumbled, grabbing the battery.

"Life is for living."

"I'm living it."

"No, you're putting off the best parts for later. When you feel you deserve it, when you feel you're ready."

He inhaled sharply.

"I'm just saying."

"Fine. So what if I am? I know what I'm doing, Violet."

She turned her beautiful dark eyes on him, then finally reached for the battery in his arms. "Here. Let me."

"I've got it."

She tried to worm her fingers under the battery, trying to take it from him. "Look at my arms, Vi. It's heavy."

She glanced at his bulging muscles, and relented. He used the distraction to stride past her, eventually plunking the battery on the counter by the cash register.

"I'll pay." She whipped out her credit card. "It's my car."

The limo ride back to his place seemed swift, and before long they were in his car, heading to Sweetheart Creek with Violet's new battery and her overnight bag, and a lot of questions whirling through his mind.

Life. Love.

What he truly wanted, as well as what he thought he deserved.

And then a few thoughts about whether during his wooing training he'd need to practice kissing Violet.

* * *

The silence in the car was a relief. It gave Violet time and space to think, to talk herself down. Leo was a nice guy, and she was starting to feel things for him, and it seemed a bit like he might be feeling some things as well. Which meant she was doing it again—seeing stuff that wasn't there. And really, who was she to flirt with him? He was a *friend*. She needed to get a grip on herself.

"Mind if I play DJ?" she asked, buying more time with her thoughts through music.

Leo nodded and gestured to his car stereo. His

T-shirt molded to him like a glove and she wondered how much he worked out. It was one of the many questions she feared asking. Because complimenting a man's physique, or at least noticing it, showed possible interest. Didn't it?

Or was she thinking too much again?

She played an ABBA song and Leo said, "I haven't heard this one in a long time." His smile warmed her gut, and she wished she'd feigned napping instead of playing music.

She chose Metallica next, figuring the cowboy wouldn't have a connection to the band or song and she would be safe from lovely smiles.

Leo laughed when the opening cords rang through his speakers. "I haven't heard this one in eons, either. I had this friend who wanted to listen to this song nonstop, all the time."

"Cowboys listen to heavy metal?"

"Some do."

"What do you think about Taylor Swift or Miley Cyrus? A fan?"

"Love them both. I actually met Miley once."

"No," she breathed. "You didn't!"

"I did. At a rodeo. She's nice." He grinned. "We exchanged autographs."

Violet shook her head. This man lived in a completely different world than she did.

The more songs she played from her teenage years, the more memories Leo shared from his own.

"I used to listen to this song on the way to rodeos," he said when she played Queen. Was there anything on her playlist that he didn't like?

"I listened to it while I studied," she replied.

"I guess it's good for getting your head in the game. Did you study a lot?"

She nodded. "Is there any music you don't listen to?"

He shrugged. "Did you like college?"

"Yeah. Do you wish you'd gone?"

He looked out the window instead of at her.

"You seem like the type who would have loved to go just for the thrill of learning something new."

He remained silent.

"Would you go now?" she pressed.

"Oh, you know." He flipped a hand off the steering wheel, a casual gesture. "Pretty busy."

"True. At least your reason for not going isn't the usual answer."

"What's that?"

"You got a gal pregnant and were busy being run out of town."

He almost choked on a burst of laughter, brightening his entire expression.

They rode, not speaking for a few more minutes, while the warm feeling in Violet's gut spread. She really enjoyed hanging out with Leo and she hoped they'd remain friends even after he found the Business Barbie of his dreams.

"Are you going to the gala next month?" he asked.

"The one Miranda was talking about in orientation?"

"Yeah, for the charity."

Violet scrunched her nose and shook her head. Black tie. A room full of wealthy people? Tons of hockey hotties? She wouldn't be able to make a peep all night.

"Why not? It's for a good cause."

"Daisy-Mae's going." The woman was head over heels for Maverick—a man so unattainable he'd declared his ranch a woman-free zone. Sure, she, Jenny and Daisy-Mae had been invited for Thanksgiving there, but that was because of his mother's influence. Despite Maverick's casual attitude, Violet had a feeling he was falling for Daisy-Mae as well. At least she hoped so.

"You can't go if she is?"

"Of course I can. I'm just not." Violet slumped in her seat.

Did she want to relive what it felt like to go to high school dances? No. She'd never been invited by a guy, and when she'd gone with friends—after sneaking out, of course because her mom thought dances would lead to trouble—she'd often sat alone because they were busy dancing. It had been awful, and she had a feeling the adult version wouldn't be much different.

But to get all dressed up and feel like a princess for one night? She longed for that. Even though she knew it was frivolous. Even though she'd been raised to know that pennies were to be saved, not poured into an expensive gown she'd wear only once.

And yet, the idea was nerve-wracking, too. To be in the same room with hockey stars and San Antonio's wealthiest members during a black-tie affair, acting like she belonged there? It made her palms sweat. But it would be good for her, too—a giant push out of her cozy comfort zone.

"It's always more fun if you have a date," Leo said.

"Have you asked Christine?"

"I told her I have a spare ticket."

Violet winced.

Leo chuckled. "I asked her nicely, I promise. I was casual. You know—played it cool. Said I had an extra ticket and would she like to come with me."

"And?"

"She's going with her sister."

"Her sister?" Violet scrunched her face. "Ouch."

"They're close."

"You mean she's Christine's shield to ward off wooing men?"

"Maybe."

"So are you going?"

"Yeah. Alone, I guess. I need to rub elbows with some mucky-mucks. Win them over with my extreme modesty and good guy charm."

"Why don't you ask someone to go as your date? If you don't want to go alone, that is."

"I don't want to go with a stranger and feel like I have to babysit her all night because she doesn't know anyone. It's easier going alone."

"Don't you worry about standing around by yourself?"

"There'll be other guys from the team there. Do you want to come with me? You can be my shield annihilator!"

"I don't have a dress."

"And I have a solution for every problem. Are you in?"

"You're going to find me a *dress*?"

"Are you in?"

"Sure. Find me a gown and a pair of shoes and I'm in. A suitable ensemble."

Leo grinned and Violet realized she had a date —a platonic one—with an NHL player to a black-tie event. And like a rags-to-riches, Cinderella kind of story, he was going to find her a dress.

Unsure what to say, Violet selected the next song from her playlist. Soon they were both bellowing the lyrics to "American Pie" with the windows down, the cab howling with the chilly November wind. Leo had a surprisingly good singing voice, a rich warm sound that seemed to wrap around her with every cord. She knew she was smiling like a crazy person, but couldn't help it. This ride was one for the memory banks.

* * *

When Leo pulled down Violet's driveway, a cat came running, its tail straight up.

"That your cat?" he asked.

"Yup."

"What's its name?"

"One."

"One?" What kind of name was that? "Starting with a *W* or with an *O*?"

"As in the number."

Leo watched Violet for a long moment, his hand still on the gearshift after he parked his car near hers. There had to be an explanation for that moniker. But she was bent over, stuffing her water bottle into the shoulder bag at her feet.

"You have to tell me the story of how he got his name," he said.

"Nothing to tell." She flashed a smile and opened her door, just about tumbling out when her foot got caught in her bag's strap.

"You're a horrible liar, Violet Granger," he declared. He was learning her tells when she was pulling his leg. Her voice rose a little higher and she tended to hide her face so her expression wouldn't give her away.

He got out, reaching for his jacket, then watched her over the car as she yanked on his locked trunk.

"Tell me."

"Pop the trunk."

"Story first."

She gave him a glare without any bite. "You really want to know?"

"Yes. Especially if there are deep, dark secrets involved."

She snorted, delighting him. It was so un-Violet to snort.

"Well, Leo." Uh-oh. There was something in her tone that made him wary, as if he'd unwittingly stepped into a stupid-man minefield. "There comes a point in every woman's life when she begins to wonder if she's going to have a family."

Yup. He really wished he hadn't pushed this one. Violet's current word: *Scary.*

And his? *Uncomfortable.*

"I've reached that point."

He nodded silently, hoping to keep himself out of trouble.

"So I decided to become a cat lady." She gestured to One, which was now winding his way between her legs in welcome. "This is the first of what will likely become many cats."

Leo wasn't sure how to respond, but had some doubt that she was serious. Violet might throw out the odd inaccurate statement here and there to get him off her case, but didn't make up stories.

"One..." he said thoughtfully.

"The next cat will be Two."

"How many will you have?"

"That's yet to be determined. Pop the trunk?"

"But you still believe in love. You want help to find… You want marriage." He shoved his fingers through his hair in confusion.

She needed him to find her someone suitable —and soon. He couldn't let her become a reclusive cat lady. She was already a quiet introvert, happy to be alone and living off the beaten path. Plus working away. And working in a costume where nobody could really see her or connect with her… It wouldn't be a long or difficult slide into the new identity of recluse.

The sound of laughter pulled him from his thoughts. "Gotcha!"

He stared at her for a moment, then blinked. She had been teasing him?

"Do I really look like someone who would freak out because I wasn't married yet?" She was at his side now, pulling on his arm.

"I don't know. Maybe. You're very private." He'd walked right into that one.

"Leo! You know me better than that."

"Remember I'm a naive man who knows very little about women when it comes to these sorts of matters. You might actually think that way. I don't know!"

He stared at her, intrigued. The more he got

to know her the more outgoing and playful she acted. Violet was bright, quick-witted and a lot of fun. He could spend a week hanging out with her without missing the rest of the world.

Her amusement softened into something more contemplative. "Sure, I want the whole package. A lot of women do. Some get it, some don't. I'm not going to throw myself off a bridge or start eating bonbons and collecting cats just because I don't get it when and how I want it."

He crossed his arms over his chest. "Okay, good."

"When the time is right, it'll all fall into place. In the meantime, I'm doing what I can to increase my opportunities."

Leo groaned. The stupid Dragon Babes thing. Didn't she realize just how dumb that idea was?

Then again, she'd pointed out that his idea to woo Christine was dumb, too.

He supposed they could be dumb together, and maybe that was part of why they clicked as friends.

"I'm working on myself and trying to let go of the things that hold me back. Maybe I'm not actually that super-responsible person who invests every dime. Maybe my habits are merely a product of my strict upbringing. Maybe I'm actually a woman who likes to buy pretty shoes she'll never wear."

"And are you?"

She sighed, looking slightly forlorn. "They hurt my feet."

He chuckled. "Well, I guess now you know, right?"

"I really resent that I spent money on them."

"Yeah?"

She pulled him toward the trunk of his car. "Now, help me become an independent woman. Show me how to replace a car battery without electrocuting myself."

How was it that when he thought he finally had Violet figured out she took a left turn? Why any of her exes had ever let her go was a mystery to him.

He hefted the new battery from his trunk, and she marched over to her car with authority, confident he would follow.

He hurried to catch up.

The cat ran alongside her, and she slowed to pick up the furry beast with the clear amber eyes. She carried it so its paws rested on her shoulder and it watched Leo with its small nose pushed deep into a patchwork of thick, dark wooly fur. The cat looked like it had tried to work on Violet's car and had the electrifying experience of failing.

"Where did One really get his name?"

"From Brant."

"Brant?" Was that her ex-fiancé? No, that was Wyatt.

"Brant Wylder. He's a vet who rescues animals around here and gives them odd names."

"So you didn't name One?"

"Nope. And One is short for Onesie."

"As in the legless T-shirt thing babies wear?"

The cat, as though sensing they were discussing him, stared at Leo with those crazy amber eyes before rubbing his head against Violet's shoulder. "He was wearing one."

Leo waited for her to say more, then finally asked, "Why?"

"His fur was matted, full of burrs and bugs. The lady who found him shaved him, but then worried he'd get a sunburn. So she put him in a onesie and called Brant to come find him a home. Apparently, One held a grudge against her after the shave."

"No doubt."

"He's still a little weird around laundry left on the floor and electric toothbrushes that make that buzzy razor sound."

"So you're not actually a cat lady?"

"Not yet." She flashed him a smile that had him wishing their day wouldn't end.

* * *

Violet tried to focus on what Leo was doing to her car. But try as she might, her attention kept straying to his hands and the flexing muscles in his forearms. He'd discarded his jacket so as not to get it dirty, and she had a pleasant view of his arms, rendering it nearly impossible to concentrate. Then again, she was focused there because when she looked up she was struck by how close together they were standing. The flecks of green in his blue eyes were mesmerizing.

It didn't help that he was strong, tanned, and confident doing mechanical things that, frankly, were beyond her comprehension.

But the mind-baffling actions weren't just limited to working on her car. He'd had all sorts of adventures that freaked her out. She liked to believe that she, too, led a life of adventure, but compared to him, her so-called big moves paled. For one, she couldn't imagine getting within six feet of a bull, let alone climbing on top of it to see how long she could stay there. And then there was his hockey career. She couldn't imagine facing off against some of the NHL's greatest players, trusting them not to hurt her as they slammed each other into the boards at high speeds.

Leo could get hurt. So hurt.

"And there you have it." He stood back and dusted his hands together. "Pretty easy."

"That's it?" she asked. It had been embarrassingly fast. If she wasn't so afraid of electricity, she could have watched an online tutorial and done this herself.

The job would have gone even faster if they hadn't had to run down to Ryan Wylder's to borrow a wrench, since Leo's had gone missing from his tool kit. Luckily, Ryan lived just across from the school, less than half a mile from her place, and had actually been home and not out with Carly Clarke on her ranch.

He'd been home, fretting over a certain piece of jewelry he planned to give his girlfriend. Ryan had held his breath as he'd shown it to Violet, seemingly worried she'd tell him it was awful. She assured him it was lovely and very much Carly's simple style.

"Want to see if it'll go?" Leo asked Violet.

Violet got behind the steering wheel and

cranked the engine. It started without a problem, but she hesitated before turning it off. She leaned out the open window to call, "Should I keep it running?"

"Nope. You should be good now."

Grinning, she rejoined him in the driveway. "Thank you. I can't believe the job was so simple."

"Next time you need something, call me before you pay a mechanic." Leo slammed the hood and leaned against the car's front panel.

"Clint has really reasonable prices."

"Good. But if the problem's small, I can teach you how to solve it yourself. It's good to know a bit about cars."

She leaned against the panel beside him, feeling the November midday sun warming her back. They'd have to return to the city in a little while for tonight's game, and Violet marveled at how fast the past fifteen hours with Leo had spun by. At the same time, last night's Thanksgiving dinner felt so long ago.

"I can't remember the last time I spent so much time with one person and didn't mind," she mused.

"True introvert, huh?"

"Sometimes. Some people are fun, but draining. Not in a bad way, though!" she said quickly.

"I just get tired." She tapped his forearm, making sure she touched fabric and not skin. No need to combust on the spot by contacting that fine, golden flesh. "You're easy to hang out with."

"Thanks. So are you."

"What do you normally do when you have time off?"

A slow grin spread across his face. "Violet Granger, are you trying a pickup line on me?"

"No!"

He laughed as she ducked her head. "You're so easy to tease. Lately, I've been helping Maverick over at his new place. It was a real wreck when he bought it."

"It seemed okay last night." The old farmhouse still needed some work, but the wood floors had obviously just been refinished and looked amazing.

"There's a reason for that. But yeah, I mostly hang out with the guys and work out. Buy groceries."

"An exciting life."

"Hey! Tell me yours is more action-packed."

She laughed. "I bake and garden. But it's November now, so mostly I bake."

"And you tease me."

"A new favorite pastime."

"What else?"

"I learned to scuba dive a few months ago," she said, eager for him to notice that she was more than a homebody waiting around for a husband. She went out and had adventures and pushed her limits sometimes.

"Really? Me, too!" He pointed to his chest. "Well, a few years ago. Next time we're near some good water, you and I should go out together. Will you be my scuba buddy?"

She almost cracked a lame joke related to a pre-dive safety check between scuba buddies, but caught herself as the joke wasn't very funny. "Um, I'd love to."

Look at that. She was already less cringey. She could flirt and tease a bit *and* catch herself before saying something lame. Hanging out with a hottie was doing wonders for her confidence.

"You will BWRAF me?" Leo said, making the scuba buddy safety check acronym sound almost like he was a little kid asking her, "You will be with me?"

"I was going to make a scuba joke, but thought it would be lame."

"Ouch!" He shifted closer, his focus on her face. "Are you calling me lame?"

"Um, yeah." She smiled briefly. "What are you going to do about it?"

The air grew quiet and their attention narrowed to just the two of them.

Leo slowly lifted a hand, reaching for her face. She tensed, certain he was going to cup her cheek and kiss her. Should she keep breathing? Stop? Close her eyes?

She wasn't ready for a kiss.

No, she was ready. And that was what freaked her out.

"You have a bit of dust here," he said. His thumb ran across her cheek, gently brushing away what must be invisible dirt, as she hadn't been anywhere near the repairs.

Violet almost ducked her head, but remembered she was trying to be bolder and braver. She held Leo's gaze, doing her best not to look away as he came closer, angled her jaw higher.

They leaned in. Her eyes drifted shut.

Meow.

Something bumped Leo, breaking his gentle grip. Onesie was nudging against him, trying to climb into Violet's arms.

The more time she spent with Leo, the more questions Violet had. And the current one was why she was a cat person.

CHAPTER 6

"Women like a man who can cook," Violet told Leo.

It had been a few weeks since he'd replaced her battery, and she was doing her best to coach him on how to get Christine's attention. Especially since their almost-kiss. Violet was afraid that if he didn't land in someone else's arms soon she'd cave and do something stupid like fall into his arms, lips puckered and ready.

Leo was adamant Christine wasn't interested in his cowboy side, and had discounted him due to it. Which meant they needed to somehow surprise her, make her reevaluate him.

"And bakers are a plus. Even though women

may act like they don't want baked goods, we secretly do. This would be a sneak attack."

"The way to a woman's heart?"

"Just like with men."

Violet went into her pantry, the old wood door creaking on its hinges. There was something about the space, with all its shelves and the scent of various ingredients, that made her think of warm kitchens on a cold winter's day, the sweet scent of butter, cinnamon and sugar baking together, and wonderful memories.

"These are from my tree." She set a large jar of peach slices on the counter. "We'll make a cobbler and you can give it to her as a Christmas gift, or a just-because gift. I've got an amazing recipe that all the ladies here in Sweetheart Creek love. They always ask me to bake a cobbler for events." She held up a warning finger. "I'm going to teach you how to make it, but if I catch you selling or sharing this recipe or making it for anyone other than Miss Pretty Perfect Princess, you're toast. Got it?"

Leo solemnly held up his right hand. "I swear."

"If she doesn't like this, then there's something seriously wrong with her."

Secretly, Violet was beginning to think there *was* something wrong with Christine. There had to be a defective gene somewhere, because how could she not be smitten with Leo? He was kind, as well as a loyal friend. Easy to hang out with. And he had his priorities straight—which, from what she'd learned, not all professional athletes did. Or at least their priorities were very different from Violet's.

So far, Leo had tried flowers, asking Christine out and doing small things for her. She clearly wasn't interested, but Leo wasn't willing to see that. Violet hoped this gift either opened Christine's heart or opened Leo's eyes.

"Not only is this a gift," Violet explained, "but it's doing something nice for her. This will show her you think of her, that you're willing to take some time from your day and make something she'd enjoy."

"Would you like it if someone baked you a cobbler?" Leo asked from his spot at the kitchen's island.

"I think every woman would—secretly. Although some might be alarmed by the gesture or wonder if you're straight." She sighed, one hand on her hip. "Honestly, we can be a strange lot, becoming suspicious of a man who bakes. But why should we? Baking is awesome. I'd love it if someone brought me baked goods."

Violet gnawed on her lip and thought about it. "Maybe this isn't a smart plan."

"I want to do it, though." He had a mischievous look in his eyes, and again Violet hesitated.

"Why? She might hate it. It could backfire, in terms of what she believes baking will say about you. This is a risky idea." Violet began putting the ingredients back in her pantry. "I'm a weird egg. I mean, how many women go out for drinks with some guy and they—"

"Barf all over your shoes?"

"Ugh. You heard?" Leo had joined her in the pantry and was studiously retrieving all the items she'd put away, returning them to the island.

"Daisy-Mae told Maverick, who mentioned it when we were working on some plumbing."

"Are you sure you still want advice from me?"

"Yes." He was in the kitchen, organizing the ingredients so he could read the labels. "The cobbler will be a test, to see how evolved she is regarding gender roles."

"Still a bad idea."

"You don't think she's evolved enough?"

"I give poor advice. Nothing has worked so far."

"It's my delivery. This..." he swept an arm

over the growing pile of ingredients "...is all in how I package and sell it to her."

"Serve it in a manly baking dish?" Violet asked, using a deep voice that made Leo smile.

"Mangled topping, and an absence of bows and gingham."

"Sorry, but the topping is always perfect. That's the beauty of lots of butter. It melts and smooths out any imperfections left by the baker. And don't tell her you made it with me. She won't enjoy hearing that."

"Okay, so I'll tell her I was thinking of her."

"Yes."

"And I was thinking of peaches..."

"No."

"Thinking of my dear sweet grandma."

"No."

"That she's too skinny and needs fattening up?"

Violet giggled.

Leo's tone turned more serious. "That I wanted to share my grandmother's most beloved dessert with her because I heard she likes peaches, too."

Violet's heart softened. "Yeah. She'll love that, even though it's technically a lie."

"Not really. My grandma baked lots of peach desserts."

"Then you're very thoughtful and sweet."

"How'd you know my two middle names?"

Laughing, Violet set to work teaching Leo how to crumble the brown sugar and butter together.

He was an efficient, enthusiastic cook, catching on quickly. His strong hands and wrists worked the butter, flour and sugar into a lovely mix for the topping.

"Cinnamon?" he announced, ceremoniously dropping a teaspoon of the spice into the bowl and sending a small scented cloud into the room. "Oops."

The counter was already dusted with other ingredients, evidence of their work.

"Are you sure you haven't baked before?" she asked as he expertly dropped dollops of topping over the waiting peach slices, then over the batch they were making for themselves.

"I watched my mom a lot. She wouldn't let me help. Said I was too messy."

Violet stepped back when he lifted the two dishes.

"Into the oven?" he asked. She opened the

door for him, sending a blast of heat into the room.

"When are you going to find a player for me?" Violet asked, as they started cleaning up their mess. So far, Leo hadn't produced a single soul.

"The best ones are taken."

She sighed. The older she got, the truer that was, it seemed.

They had a cup of tea while they waited for the cobblers to brown. Before long, they were scooping vanilla ice cream over steaming bowls of peaches and their wonderful, crispy and soft topping.

Violet closed her eyes as she took the first bite. "Mmm."

She glanced over as Leo tasted his. His brows curved upward and he quickly shoveled more into his mouth. "So good!"

Laughing, they ate until there was nothing left of their dish.

"Don't tell the team's dietician!" Leo stated.

"I won't. Besides, Athena would never believe we ate the whole thing." Violet grasped her stomach and leaned back. "Wow, I'm so full."

"I can't believe how much you packed away." Leo bent to look under the table. "Where did you put it all?"

"Trust me. It's all in my stomach." She groaned. "I need to stop at one helping."

"It's not your fault. This stuff is irresistible." Leo eyed the dish they'd made for Christine. "Think Christine would mind if we ate hers, too? Because this stuff is seriously the way to someone's heart, and right now I'm falling hard."

* * *

"So? Is Christine yours forever? You didn't text me!" Violet fell into step beside Leo as they walked from the parking lot to the arena. It had been several days since they'd baked cobbler together, and with an out-of-town game thrown into the mix he hadn't managed to bring her up to speed.

"Sorry." In fact, as much as he hated to admit it, he'd been avoiding her, not wanting to tell her what had happened. He was losing faith in his plan, and without the woo-Christine strategy where would he be with Violet? Would she want to hang out as often if they didn't have the common goal of training him to act like he was in love?

Man, when he thought of it that way, it seemed really messed up.

"Oh, no." She stopped walking, her expression stricken. "She can't tolerate gluten? Why didn't I think of that?"

Leo stopped as well, tipped his head back and sighed. Violet had worked so hard to help him. How could he admit he was ready to give up? But how could he keep moving forward when his heart wasn't in it any longer?

It was so easy being with Violet. And with Christine…it wasn't. Why couldn't he just hang out with Violet all the time and have his life unfold in the way he envisioned it? He'd worked hard for so many years with barely a rest. He was tired and wanted to enjoy where he was, but how could he? He didn't have what he needed in order to securely start a family.

Christine was still the answer. The two of them were compatible in that they were focused on the future and not on emotions. Little risk and all benefit.

And yet they weren't clicking.

Violet rested a hand on his arm. "What happened?"

"Nothing."

"Don't clam up on me."

"Seriously, *nothing*."

"Nothing?"

143

Leo sighed.

"You don't look like a man who gave away my prized cobbler to the woman of your affections. Unless you're *tired*. Did she thank you in a very *personal* kind of way?" She elbowed him with a sly grin that made him laugh. Until he thought of the reception he'd had from Christine. She was not evolved enough to appreciate baked goods from a man, and there had been no intimate thank you, that was for certain.

"She didn't try it."

"What?" Violet was standing in front of him now, hands on her hips. He almost laughed at her expression. She was like a pit bull, ready to jump on his enemies and defend him. "Why not?"

"She's off sugar and wheat and unhealthy fats, and everything good in this world."

"Good things like you."

"Yeah," he said softly.

They walked into the arena, the security guard nodding at them as they flashed their staff passes. "Have a good game tonight, y'all," he drawled.

"Thanks, man," Leo replied.

"Shouldn't this all be easier? I mean, if she's the right one, it should be simple." Leo stopped several feet later to open a second door that would give them access to the locker rooms.

Violet stared at him, and in that moment he would have given up his contract to get her take on what he was feeling and what he should do about it.

He wanted to skip the complicated, distracting romance and inevitable fights he'd heard about from his friends. He wanted a partnership like his parents had. They had the right idea. Work hard, raise your family, go out for a game of Bridge once in a while.

Simple. They were coming up on forty years in just a few days and he'd be flying out to celebrate with them.

That was what he wanted.

"I'm not a good coach." Violet sighed, looking defeated. "I mean, we should have seen this coming. She wears designer clothes and lives in a world I don't at all understand. I fear I've mucked up your chances with her."

"But why didn't she at least try our cobbler?" Leo held in his frustration. Christine had been surprised by the gift. It was thoughtful and homemade. Just as Violet had instructed. But Christine hadn't immediately dug into it like he'd expected, hadn't even taken a few polite bites. She'd looked at it, smiled sweetly, then sent it back home with him.

"Not even a bite?" Violet groaned and clapped her palms to her face. "You have to stop listening to me."

"No way." He tugged her hands from her cheeks. "I need you. You warned me this was a bad idea."

"Whatever my first instinct is, you should do the opposite. Christine and I are poles apart. She's glamorous and famous and has this amazing job,"

"No, *my* instincts are wrong."

"Pretty sure mine are."

"The women I grew up around ate whatever. It's like I don't even know or understand Christine…" He paused, thinking over his confession. Why was he pursuing her if he didn't know her? Was it enough that she lent the right image and that he believed she would help him get where he wanted to be?

Weren't there people you could hire to help you market yourself?

Why was he trying so hard to get Christine Lagrée to see his potential?

Because she knew sports and was connected to the same world he was, just in a different way. He knew they could help each other.

But it wasn't happening.

"Ranchers burn off tons of calories working on their land," Violet said, still arguing that he wasn't in the wrong, it was her.

But if that was true, it was likely because of him and his stupid plan to woo a woman who couldn't see past his cowboy roots.

"You eat cobbler," he pointed out.

"I do."

"And you don't work on a ranch."

"Also true."

"Maybe Christine is defective."

Perhaps that could be her word. Although maybe when he was around it was simply *uninspired*.

Violet gave a snort-laugh. "She's not defective. She's very nice."

"I'm starting to think I don't understand women at all. This is hopeless."

Violet touched his arm. "Hey, you understand me, and I'm not a rancher. Don't beat yourself up." Her voice turned gentle. "I hate to say it, but maybe the two of you just aren't compatible or meant to be. You're not her type."

"How is that even possible? Have you looked at me?" He shot Violet a grin and she laughed.

"There's that down-home modesty shining through again."

"Come here," he said, opening his arms. He could use a hug right now. Not only to ward off the crappy feeling of failure, but to thank Violet for being such an awesome, loyal friend.

She blinked, then tentatively curved her body against his for a hug there in the chilly hallway. He sighed, releasing the tension from his body and mind. Hugging Violet made everything feel doable again. Maybe even attempting to woo Christine one last time. She did laugh at his jokes and return his text messages, at least. So maybe it wasn't entirely hopeless.

"Where's the cobbler? Need help eating it?" Violet leaned back and looked up at him. "Tell me you didn't leave it with her so she could toss it as soon as you were gone."

"Not a chance."

"So?" She stepped back, breaking that warm, delicious contact. He hadn't realized how beat-up he'd been feeling and how much he'd needed that hug from a friend. Her support was always the best. But hugs? You couldn't top them. Especially the way Violet's petite body packed a punch that would knock the wind out of you if you let her.

"Cobbler?" Violet repeated. "We can pick up ice cream on the way home."

He shot her a guilty look.

"What?"

"I already ate it."

She gave a bark of laughter. "You lie! You're hiding it somewhere so you can have it all to yourself."

Leo chuckling, ducked her playful shove. "Why do you think I sucked on the ice during the last away game? I ate it all."

"No." Violet breathed the word, her tone incredulous. "*All* of it? The whole thing?"

"Don't tell Athena I veered off the diet plan."

"Veered? You ate almost two entire cobblers in what—three days? You smashed her plan into a guardrail and over the cliff."

He gave a sheepish smile. "They were really good."

They began walking side by side again, almost at the locker rooms. "Two cobblers? And after you gave Maverick and Dylan such a hard time about eating dessert at Thanksgiving, here you are binging like nobody's looking."

"Moment of weakness. We all have 'em."

"Did Coach Louis say anything about your skating?"

"He subbed me so fast I think he noticed. But he was smiling."

"Smiling? He didn't even rip you a new one about the team needing a win or something?"

"Nope. He's been a bit odd since he moved back to Sweetheart Creek a few weeks ago."

"Do you think he's in love?"

Leo laughed. "Louis? No way."

The day his coach fell was the day he would, as well. Never going to happen.

* * *

Leo looked around the familiar old farmhouse kitchen. Somehow, it seemed brighter than it had when he was a kid. And his parents appeared happier, too. Less burdened and preoccupied.

Was it because their kids had moved out and were somewhat established in their adult lives, so they could focus on themselves? Or was it because they had friends and family here to celebrate with them tonight? Or because their ranch was in a good place financially?

He figured it was likely the latter, and he was grateful he'd been a part of helping them achieve it.

He grabbed the plate of nachos he'd been sent to retrieve and returned to the living room, which was brimming with friends and neighbors who'd come out to celebrate his parents' fortieth wedding anniversary.

While he'd been growing up, his folks had barely celebrated their own birthdays, let alone an anniversary. It was nice to see them so happy, and definitely worth squeezing in the flight between game days. But it was also unexpected.

Setting the nachos on the food table, he went to stand beside his mom, Jenny-Lee. "What made you two decide to celebrate this year?"

"Because we can."

"Then why not the others?"

She shrugged, doing one of those familiar frown-smile things she did. "We were too busy with the ranch and keeping our heads above water. We were also raising a bunch of hooligans." She winked at him.

"Right. Business comes first."

"We let our relationship sit on the back burner for a long time. Too long."

"You have a partnership first and foremost," he said, letting her know he understood.

She gave him a strange look.

"It's smart," he said.

The frown was back, deepening with every word he spoke.

"When you run a business or a brand...you

don't need distractions," he insisted, waiting for her to agree.

His mom was really studying him now, with a sort of curious expression similar to one he saw on Violet's face when they talked about these things.

"I hope you're not taking what you saw us doing and using it as relationship advice." Her tone was stern.

"But…" He gestured to the banner someone had painted that said Congratulations on 40 Years!

They'd made it. What they'd done worked.

Jenny-Lee squeezed his arm. "A relationship has to be nurtured. You can't neglect it."

He gestured to the banner again.

"Come with me." She dragged him back to the kitchen, where she pointed to the table. "Sit."

He grabbed a chair, and she collected the ceramic cat cookie jar from the counter, then joined him at the table like old times. He took two of her homemade oatmeal raisin cookies, savoring the sweet cinnamon taste. It made him think of baking cobblers with Violet.

His mom took a cookie for herself and plunked the jar on the table between them.

"A lot of our time went into the business when

you were younger. So much was riding on it and we were too exhausted at the end of the day to put effort into our relationship."

He nodded. He remembered those years, the exhaustion and strain.

"We considered separating a few years ago."

"What? Why?" They'd been inseparable. It had driven him nuts, seeing the lack of efficiency when they'd both work on the same job together instead of dividing and conquering the ranch's never-ending to-do list.

Wait. *Time.* It was one of the things Violet had listed. Maybe spending time together was a way they expressed their love for each other.

His mom's smile was sad. "A lot of reasons."

"Name one."

"Because our son, who was supposed to be going out into the world and making his own way, had one foot stuck on the ranch, which was pulling him down."

Leo looked his mom dead in the eye and said, "And I would do it all again."

"I know. But no son should ever have to sacrifice like that. For a while, at the beginning, your dad was holding on to the money you were sending, planning to give it back to you. We came really close to letting the bank foreclose."

"You didn't want the help?"

"No parent would ever wish to need to be bailed out by their kid. It's…"

Humiliating. Humbling. Shameful, even. He'd never thought how they might feel about his help, had only thought of how they'd feel if they'd been turfed off their land.

"Your name is on the deed."

"What?" How would they get that past the lawyers and banks without his knowledge? Could you even do that?

His mom reached across the table, laid her hand over the one still holding his forgotten cookie. "It was give it to you or to the bank."

"Yeah, don't give it to the bank."

"Your dad decided that if this place meant that much to you, it should be yours. Your money, your asset. We're just taking care of it for you."

"What? No. It's *yours*, Mom. Yours and Dad's."

"We were going to discuss this tomorrow before you fly out." Her eyes were damp.

"Why did you decide to stay?"

"Because this land is part of our family history. It's in our blood. Could you imagine growing up anywhere else but here?"

He shook his head.

"It wasn't just about you kids. It was about us

a bit, too."

"What do you mean?"

"Who am I without the ranch? Who is your dad? The idea of leaving the land sent him into a depression." She laughed and pulled her hand away, leaving Leo's feeling cold and abandoned. "Could you see the two of us working for someone else? Their terms, their schedule. Or even just see us sitting at a desk all day?"

He shook his head wryly. At one point early in his rodeo career he'd agreed to a short contract to help a saddle company with some marketing. He hadn't realized how much time he'd be sitting be-hind a computer, learning spreadsheets. He'd lasted four days.

"So here you are."

"Here we are." She opened her hands.

He leaned forward. "I hope your names are on the deed as well, because the amount I sent doesn't cover even half the value."

"We learned to celebrate what we have. See the abundance amid scarcity. The idea of losing all this reminded me and your father why we're here. What made us good together. We had to find a way to re-appreciate it all. Including each other. You know your dad and I were high school sweethearts?"

Leo knew they'd started dating in high school, but the word *sweetheart* had never been used to describe their relationship. It had been more a story of how they'd both had the same plans for ranch life, family and kids.

"We could see how our life was going to unfold after graduation. And I knew I'd have my best friend at my side. It was wonderful. It helped us through so many tough times."

Leo thought of all the things his parents had gone through, the looks they used to share at the end of the day, that unspoken language they had. Was that their friendship speaking?

"Did you hear we're going to spend three weeks in the Caribbean?"

"The Caribbean? Do you even own bathing suits?"

She laughed. "We've always wanted to go, so we rented a little beach hut along the water. We're going to sit there and enjoy each other's company."

"For three weeks?" No cattle to check on or feed. Just sit and talk. He couldn't see it.

"For three weeks." Jenny-Lee grinned. "It's time me and my love had some time just for ourselves."

Me and my love?

Where were the parents he knew?

And he had shares in this ranch?

He wasn't sure how all of this new knowledge changed his world, but he was fairly confident that it would.

"Don't give me that look," his mom said with a laugh.

"What look?"

"You know your dad and I love each other very much. Marriage isn't some platonic business deal. We would have never made it through the hard times without some pretty deep love for each other."

"But..." Leo closed his eyes, trying to summon all his thoughts into one question. "How did you manage to stay together for all these years if you weren't doing those little things that tell each other you love them?"

"Maybe we were, and it wasn't for you to see." She gave him a look that suggested he mind his own business, then got up, taking the cookie jar, and laughed at his baffled expression. Leaning forward, she whispered, "Bridge night."

"What about it?"

"Neither of us knows how to play."

CHAPTER 7

*D*id Leo believe in romantic, heart-wrenching, heart-stopping love? The question had been plaguing him since Violet had asked him about love back in November, in the limo. Only a month ago, but it felt like eons.

He believed he couldn't fall in love. It wasn't what he was looking for—that big romantic moment when you "just knew" that the other person was the one for you. And that your life wouldn't be complete without them sharing jokes and adventures.

That sounded like a partnership to him, and he hadn't once thought that love was the ideal.

But now, after talking to his mom, and trying to pursue Christine Lagrée and failing, he wondered if he had it all backward. Maybe love and friendship—a full partnership—was the needed foundation. And love wasn't a mere bonus that might complicate the relationship or hold him back from his dreams.

It felt crazy that he could ever think that love and friendship weren't important pieces of the partnership puzzle when it came to marriage. And maybe Christine sensed that? Maybe that's why she kept him at arm's length? Or maybe because she didn't see love ever happening between them, and like Violet, was looking for it.

It was all so confusing. He wanted a plan, a strategy, and it felt like he was trying to lasso a cloud.

Shaking his head, he walked up the steps to Violet's charming former B and B. He'd told her he couldn't—didn't—fall in love. Didn't believe in it. How could he be so preoccupied with living that he didn't understand life?

He straightened his tuxedo jacket and glanced over his shoulder at the limousine idling in the chilly December evening air. Violet had been so delighted with the other limo that he'd hired one for tonight's Dragons gala. She'd tried to insist they meet up in the city, but he'd pulled the

Boyfriend Practice card and said he'd pick her up. Their ride, however, was a surprise.

He smiled, thinking of her delight the first time she'd ridden in a limousine. How her long fingers had glided over the leather surfaces, how tickled she'd been discovering the hidden compartments. It had made him question why he was being so frugal. Sure, he had plans for his future that included full financial freedom within a few years, but why did he have to be so stingy with himself? He was limiting his life experiences, and he was in a position where he could spend a bit without throwing himself off his stringent plan.

Plus, he was also part owner of a Montana ranch. That thought made him smile. He shared the land his family worked. It felt good. Really good. *Breathing room.* That's what his grandfather had called that feeling.

That didn't mean his plans had changed, though. He still wanted to be financially independent before he started a family. He wanted to be there for his kids and wife and know that, no matter what happened, he had enough to get them through any of life's hiccups or bumps without having to go back to work somewhere away from them.

He believed in love. All forms of it.

And he was starting to believe that a life without it would be gray and lacking.

He knocked on the peach-colored door with the cute stained-glass panel. When he was ready to settle down, he could see himself living in a modest place with impeccable charm like this. He'd hang a swing from the large oak growing beside the house. Maybe build a tree fort in that spot where the branches met, just high enough off the ground that you'd feel like the king of the world.

But best of all, there would be no banks that came knocking, threatening to take it all.

Violet opened the door and he froze, all thoughts of bankers and tree forts whisked away. Looking at her, any man would believe in love. She was drop-dead, eat your own tie gorgeous. So beautiful it hurt to look at her.

No, scrap that. It didn't hurt. But it brought on a feeling that was foreign and weird. A tugging in his gut, drawing him closer to her, shutting out everything around him other than her.

"You look gorgeous," he said. He cleared his throat, removing the huskiness.

"Thank you," she said, fumbling with her purse and a coat as she turned to lock her front door. She'd draped an off-white cashmere shawl-thing over her shoulders, contrasting with her black strapless gown. His panda bear was in black and white again. The dress hugged her every curve, showcasing her petite frame. Her straight black hair was pulled up in some sort of twist, and was speckled with small sparkly gems. He tried to get closer to see how they stayed in place, but she turned, bumping against his chest.

"Oh," she said softly. "Hello."

"You smell nice."

She stared at him for a long, heavy second while he recovered. He leaned in to place a kiss on her cheek. He'd never kissed a woman hello before and he moved slowly, afraid she'd make a sudden move and they'd bump heads. His lips landed against her cheek and he savored the softness, the scent of her hair, her skin, and the way her small intake of breath stilled his heart.

She didn't move until he leaned back.

He slowly held out his arm for her to take. He couldn't seem to look away from the smoky effect she'd dusted around her dark eyes. She was mysterious.

He nearly stumbled when the first step down caught him off guard. He gave a brief smile, glancing away long enough to calculate where next to place his feet.

He'd barely seen Violet over the past several weeks, keeping himself busy as he sorted out his thoughts. They'd texted and bumped into each other at work and at the Dragons' first charity event on the children's ward. But he'd basically been avoiding her.

At the same time, whenever he'd help with work at Maverick's house, just a few miles from hers, he always offered to make the coffee runs into town, hoping for a chance encounter.

"A limo?" Violet said softly, as they made their way down the front path to where it was parked, the driver waiting by its back door.

"Boyfriends do things that delight their girl-friends. Gifts, right? Or does this go under the category of doing nice and thoughtful things?"

She looked at him, her eyes wide and indecipherable.

"You liked the other limo, right? Did I pick up on the correct cues?"

"Yes, of course. Very thoughtful." She placed a hand against his cheek before she got into the car. "Christine doesn't know what she's missing."

Leo slid onto the seat beside her, thanking the driver as he shut the door.

It felt different being in the limo with the two of them dressed up. It wasn't a lark, like the first time. Now it felt as though they were playing a part, and a current was zipping between them.

"You made me realize limo rides are fun," he said, breaking the silence. "And I have enough money to rent one. So why not?"

Violet's cheeks turned pink and her chin dipped down. "Thank you for the dress."

"You bet." He cleared his throat. He'd sent her into a store in the city to choose her outfit for tonight. It had felt odd, calling their staff to request she be able to put whatever she desired on his card. But he'd also felt proud of being able to return a helpful favor for a friend in a way that would make her feel special. "Goes with the limo, right?"

"And the limo is because we drive beaters and we'd be teased without mercy if we showed up at the gala driving them."

He laughed. "No way. You just park around the block."

"You do that?"

He shrugged again.

"Why don't you just buy a new car? I'm sure there's a dealership in the city that would love to have you as a customer. Maybe a Jag?"

"My dad would kill me."

"Really?"

Leo shook off the image of his father's disapproving face if he showed up in a car worth that much. He was pretty sure the man would come up with a long list of more important things his son could have bought instead of the status symbol.

But maybe it was time to pull a Violet and do something out of character just to see if he was playing out the habits of his upbringing. Like her and the fancy shoes. He'd buy a snazzy car and see if he liked it. And who knows? Maybe his dad would be proud.

Violet was smoothing her fingers along the soft fabric of her dress. He could see how much she loved it, and it made him happy that he'd thought to set her up with the shopping trip. He had a feeling her gown was like his first tailored suit—the kind of outfit that made you feel strong, confident and good-looking. The guys had razzed him about his off-the-rack suits until he'd relented and allowed Maverick's tailor to set him up with a suit, as well as a tux for tonight. He'd nearly fainted when he got the bill.

"I appreciate the fancy ride and this lovely dress."

"But?"

"You know you don't need to overspend when it comes to me."

"I needed a date. Tonight I woo Family Zone."

"And Christine."

"I'd like to be in a movie. Or on a billboard. Maybe a commercial or two... I'm not fussy." He winked. "And you're my wingman. "

She let out a shuddery huff that almost sounded like a laugh. "A wingman who continually clams up. I'm going to be absolutely no help."

"Knowing you have my back and are cheering me on is huge." He clasped her hand and gave it a squeeze. "I appreciate you coming with me. Besides, you don't really seem to clam up much any longer."

"True."

As they drove back through Sweetheart Creek to get to the highway, Violet shifted forward in her seat to peer at a group of people gathered on Main Street in front of an empty shop across from the diner. The windows were covered in newspaper, except for one where the yellowed paper had been removed.

"What's Jackie up to now?" Violet muttered. "And Henry? Mrs. Fisher? And is that Hannah?"

Leo tapped on the glass divider separating

them from the driver, and it lowered. "Slow down, please."

Violet was still muttering under her breath about weird occurrences and the end of times.

"Want to stop?" he asked her, puzzled about what was going on.

She leaned back in her seat. "Nah. I'm just being a snoop. I'm sure I'll hear all about whatever this is soon enough." She peered through the window again as the limo crawled along. "Maybe Hannah is opening her own day care or something."

The small group in front of the store turned, watching the car. Leo asked the driver to stop.

"Come on," he said. He opened his door before the man could come around, and reached for Violet's hand.

"No way." She gestured to her fancy outfit. "We have to get to the gala and I'm just being nosy."

"That's exactly why we need to stop."

She rolled her eyes.

"Come on," he coaxed. "Be curious, Vi. I don't mind. Besides, you look beautiful. Show yourself off a little." He knew she wouldn't quite believe just how amazing she was from the inside on out until it was reflected back to her by her own world.

* * *

Mrs. Fisher squealed, her hands performing a jittery dance as she hustled up to Violet on the sidewalk, her red-and-gold Christmas-garland earrings swinging. She embraced Violet in a hug, surrounding her with the scents of coffee and bacon. "Oh, sweetheart! Look at you." Clasping her shoulders, she held Violet out in front of her, taking in her gown.

Her friend Jackie Moorhouse grinned at her. "You're hotter than a black leather interior in hundred-and-ten-degree heat with no air-conditioning."

Mrs. Fisher turned to Leo. "Don't y'all just melt looking at this woman?"

"I do."

The sincerity in his voice made Violet's cheeks burn.

"She's going to be the most beautiful woman at the gala tonight," he said.

Okay, going too far. She gave him a dry look, the spell broken. "Daisy-Mae's going to be there."

"Oh, I bet she'll look like she stepped out of a magazine," the older woman gushed.

"Not my type, Mrs. Fisher," Leo said easily.

"Christine Lagrée is his type," Violet stated, feeling a strange wringing sensation in her chest at the thought of Leo finally capturing the woman he'd been pursuing for several months.

Hannah gasped. "She's gorgeous!"

Violet nodded, knowing Leo was starting to have doubts about Christine. She hoped that tonight she could show him that he didn't need a loveless relationship, and could find career advancement in something a bit less old-fashioned than a marriage geared to that. She had seen the RSVP list and knew who to introduce him to. She just had to be quick and not think, or she'd clam up. She needed to show him he could receive help when it came to finding success and happiness—without tying himself into a loveless relationship.

Jackie, eyes wide, mouthed the word *hot* to Violet, tipping her head in Leo's direction. Violet introduced the two, then quietly pointed out Henry Wylder, the great-uncle of the Wylder brothers, to Leo. He was scowling through the dusty window of the building, and she decided he was a lot like the local armadillo, Bill. Best not disturbed.

Mrs. Fisher waved a hand. "You're never getting Christine, Leo. She's not gonna fall for a cowboy like y'all."

Violet giggled as Leo glanced down at his very classy, not-at-all-Western tuxedo. "For what it's worth, I'm starting to believe I have a thing for women with dark hair and mysterious eyes," he mused.

Violet giggled again when Hannah sighed, but stopped when Leo winked at her, his gaze lingering just long enough that she couldn't quite brush off his words.

Was she projecting her own feelings onto him, seeing what she wanted to see, like she had with Owen? She knew he was just flirting, playing the role of the adoring date in front of her friends to make her feel good. He wasn't flirting in hopes of their friendship becoming more.

She just had to remember that.

"And what about me?" Leo asked, striking a pose. "Don't I look good?"

"Very nice," Hannah and Jackie said together.

Violet had barely allowed herself to look at him. He was so gorgeous. A cowboy in a tuxedo? It was like her knees didn't remember how to work properly.

But now she drank him in, from his freshly

styled hair to those devilish eyes that charmed her with secret tales she felt only she could translate. The jacket was cut to showcase the width of his shoulders, the power hidden beneath the fine woven cloth. The pants hung from his hips as if their designer saw him the way a hungry woman would.

"Did Maverick's tailor do me right?" he asked.

He sure did. There was no doubt. Even when styles changed and women looked back on photos of tonight, they'd know that this man's tailor knew what he was doing.

"He did okay," Violet said casually. She was definitely crushing on the man, but there was no way she was letting on how sexy he was. Especially since her friend Leo seemed to be well versed in practicing the things women liked, and all the particular things that made her heart beat a little faster.

Truly, it was quite unfair.

While Leo played up his wounded ego for Jackie and Mrs. Fisher, Violet moved to the shop's dirty window. "What's going on in there?"

She tried to peer inside without brushing her dress against the grimy exterior, the peeling paint, but couldn't see a thing.

"Coffee shop. With fresh baked goods." Mrs.

Fisher looked more tense than on auction day, when the Longhorn Diner was filled to the rafters with impatient, hungry customers.

"Bookstore," Jackie said, authority ringing in her voice.

"No, no. You're both wrong," Henry proclaimed. "It's a toy store—"

"A toy store will never make it here," Violet interrupted. "I was hoping you were starting your own day care, Hannah."

She furiously shook her head, eyes wide.

"*And* it's a speakeasy," Henry said gruffly. "I say we run 'em out of town before they get started."

"A speakeasy toy store?" Leo said doubtfully as he stepped to the window.

"That makes no sense, Henry," Violet told him.

"I'm just saying that's what's on the permit." He pointed to a document taped to the glass.

"It says nothing about a speakeasy," Leo stated. "It says retail."

"It's a speakeasy. Mark my words, this'll be the end of the town!"

Jackie rolled her eyes, but Mrs. Fisher's shoulders stiffened and she pulled her puffy jacket tighter around her. "I need to get back to my diners." She gave Violet's arm a squeeze. "Enjoy tonight, sweetie." She sent Leo an extra-long look of approval. "Promise me you won't be good."

Violet laughed. "We're just friends!"

Sadly.

"Y'all should come to a football game with me in September," Jackie said, winking at Violet.

Violet smiled, wishing her friend's match-making prowess could work on her. Anyone she took to a football game seemed to be happily married within a year or two.

Either way, Violet wished Leo would begin to believe in love, now that he was starting to see that he shouldn't have to try so hard with Christine if it was meant to be.

"I brought you a glass of champagne," Leo said, passing Violet the flute he'd snagged for her. He'd left her chatting with Daisy-Mae, but saw that Violet was now alone, standing near one of the many tall Christmas trees that decorated the grand ballroom. Leaving her alone was something he'd promised he wouldn't do if she came with him tonight. "Sorry I was gone so long. When did Daisy-Mae leave?"

"Feeling guilty about abandoning me?"

"Very much so. Would it help if I told you you're a stunning wallflower?"

"Cheers to that." She tapped her flute lightly against his highball glass. "What are you drinking?"

"Tonic water."

"Did you know it contains quinine, which is used to help treat malaria?"

Leo looked at the clear liquid. "Really? Is it safe for me to have a couple, or will I overdose on something?"

Violet shrugged, her bare shoulders lifting. Her light brown skin with the faint reddish undertones was smooth and irresistible. Leo gently brushed one of the longer tendrils of hair off her neck, and she shivered as his fingers grazed her skin.

"You had a little something there," he lied. He lightly touched the elbow holding her champagne. "Want to dance?"

"I thought you were here to make deals with some mucky-mucks?"

She was watching the crowd in that serious way he'd noticed earlier. All night she'd been acting like more of a networking social butterfly than he'd assumed she'd ever be comfortable being. She had made several quick, strategic introductions, and had even occasionally eavesdropped on nearby conversations, then joined in, drawing Leo with her. So far, he'd met a lot of corporate heads. It was as though Violet had studied the guest list before their arrival and was determined to be the woman he wanted Christine to be.

Which was kind of funny, seeing as they weren't looking to move their friendship into something more than it was.

"You've been working hard. I believe a break is in order." He reached for her glass with plans to abandon it, even though it was still full. Violet took a sip, then allowed him to set it aside as the orchestra began a new tune.

She hooked her fingertips in his with a featherlight touch that sent tingles up to his elbow. On the dance floor, she floated into his arms, and he inhaled her scent. Her waist and lower back were small under the span of his hand and she was scented with something he couldn't quite identify. Rosemary? Lavender? Whatever it was, he found it soothing and relaxing, like her. He couldn't help but hope that his tuxedo smelled of her when he got home tonight.

They easily fell into step, dancing almost as if they'd taken lessons together. Who would have thought it? A cowboy and a wallflower could tear up the dance floor to an orchestra's slow beat.

"Thank you for introducing me to so many people," he said.

She smiled, the strings of lights above the dance floor creating twinkling highlights in her glossy black hair and making the small gems twinkle. He reached up to touch one. They seemed to be glued to her hair.

"You don't seem shy tonight," he said.

She gave a small shrug, interrupting their rhythm, and he gripped her tighter to prevent her from tumbling. She was suddenly so close, sharing the heat that was building between them.

Before tonight he'd noticed that she was pretty, but he'd never realized just how beautiful.

"What's your secret?" Leo asked.

"I'm just being a good friend."

"You're always a good friend."

"And I'm practicing being less reserved and self-conscious and shy." Her face had gone red, the hand on his shoulder trembling slightly, her lower lip clamped between her teeth.

"Well, thank you. For pushing beyond your comfort zone to try and help me. I appreciate it."

She relaxed, and their steps took on an easy rhythm again.

"Have I been a good practice-boyfriend tonight?" He'd put thought into the limo and setting her up with something to wear as promised, but beyond that had slipped into autopilot, thinking more about career moves than her.

She nodded. "Very good."

She wouldn't meet his gaze, and he wished she'd stop searching out whoever she wanted to introduce him to next, and focus on him.

"Have I hit all five of the good boyfriend habits?"

"You don't have to hit all five with me," she said absently.

"But practice. I want to be good at this." For some reason it felt extra important to ace this tonight, like he was writing his final exam.

"You're fine."

"What can I do to make your night better?"

Her lips parted and her eyes finally met his. She seemed unable to speak, her cheeks flushing with color.

"Now you're going to be shy? Right here? With me?" He crinkled his nose at her, trying to loosen the shyness that seemed to have her in its grip.

The song ended, and they stopped swaying. Eventually, Leo realized he should release her from his embrace. He cleared his throat and guided her to the side of the dance floor, suddenly feeling awkward.

"If anyone bids higher on this, put your name down." Maverick Blades waved a sheet of paper in front of Leo, tapping it impatiently.

"What is this?"

"I'll pay you back later. I need to win this blanket."

"Uh? What?"

Maverick pointed a finger at Leo. "You got my back?"

"Um, sure. Of course."

His friend's shoulders eased, and he went to return the silent auction bidding sheet to one of the long tables lined with items.

"What's with you and Dak tonight, man?" Leo asked, automatically following him. First, he'd found Dak, the team's head charity dude, in the bathroom, basically standing up his date, who'd been looking for him all night. Now Maverick was getting all squirrelly and stressed out about some knitted blanket.

If this was love, count him out. It looked stressful. Not at all what Leo had been imagining over the past few weeks.

Maverick shot him a warning look. "Just do it, Socks."

Leo grumbled at the nickname the team had given him for "losing" his socks before their first exhibition game of the season. He was still certain he'd been the victim of a prank. "Fine."

Violet had wandered off and was checking out the auction's tables. He caught up with her, asking, "Anything catch your eye?"

He passed a jersey signed by the entire team. Seeing his name scrawled on the fabric beside big names like Maverick's still felt odd. He'd looked up to these players for so long his brain still hadn't caught up to the fact that he was now one of them.

"Check this out." Violet pointed to a getaway to a South Carolina beach town called Indigo Bay.

"What is it?" He bent over the table, reading the bidding sheet. It offered an overnight in a resort's ocean-side cottage, and included scuba diving.

"No way," he said. "Are you going to bid on it?"

Violet shook her head. "It's already at $1700."

"Does that include airfare?" Indigo Bay was about a twenty-hour drive from their part of Texas.

She shook her head again.

Leo did some rough mental calculations. You could probably get the same package for less by booking directly. But two people? Beach-side cottage *and* scuba? He scrawled his name on the sheet with a bid of $1800.

"If you win, you have to take me with you," Violet said, clasping his arm.

"Sorry, already told Sara-Lynn I'd bring her." He gave a hapless shrug as though to say, "What can you do?"

"You haven't had time to contact your sister, *and* she doesn't scuba," Violet said, narrowing her eyes.

"How would you know?"

"We chat on the phone every night."

"Do not."

Violet gave him a smile best described as devious.

"You don't." She didn't. There was no way. They'd never even met. No, wait. There was that time his family had come to one of his games and had swarmed Violet afterward. They'd adored her and threatened to bring her home with them, Sara-Lynn in particular. How had he forgotten that?

"I get to go with you." She held up her little

finger as if she was asking for a pinkie swear to seal the deal.

"I am not six years old," he said, crossing his arms, staring at her raised finger with the peachy-pink-painted nail.

"Christine!" Violet said, her voice lifting. "Gorgeous dress."

"Thank you." The blonde moved closer, her black gown a clingy affair that was like a shout-out to good genetics, healthy eating and a personal trainer.

"Yes, very lovely," Leo said absently. Christine Lagreé's gaze raked over him, and he turned back to Violet, muttering, "I'm not taking you."

"Of course you are," she muttered under her breath, smile still in place. She sent a pointed look in Christine's direction.

Right. He turned back to her. "Can I get you a drink?"

She waved the full champagne glass in her hand.

Perfect.

He turned back to Violet, still working over the did-she-actually-chat-with-his-sister question. "What would you and Sara-Lynn even talk about?"

"Do you scuba dive?" Violet asked Christine,

181

pushing him aside so he wasn't standing between the two of them.

"No way," she replied, her brow wrinkling. "Scuba's way too scary." She shuddered.

"It's not as bad as you might imagine," Violet said. "Leo's bidding on a package for two. I thought if he won—"

"I already told Violet I'm taking my sister," he insisted.

"You don't take your sister on a romantic getaway!"

"And you don't take your best friend, either."

Violet gave an indignant huff, although he saw the way she lit up at being called his best friend. Leo shot her a sassy, you-can't-tell-me-what-to-do look and changed his bid to $2000.

"What are you doing?" She yanked the pen from his grip, but he snatched it back, along with the clipboard.

"You're interfering with fund-raising." He looked around for one of the volunteers, who were dressed as Santa's elves. "This woman is preventing me from bidding!"

"You're so immature!" Violet jabbed him with a finger. *"And* bad with money." She gestured to the form, where he'd outbid himself.

"It's for *charity*," he said, leaning in close, and breathing in her scent again.

They stared at each other for a long beat, her nearly-black eyes appearing almost a milk-chocolate brown as indignation flashed, then faded.

I'd take you with me.

He blinked at the unexpected thought and spun away as if he'd been shocked by Violet. He dropped the pen and clipboard and inhaled with a shudder. To find Christine staring at him, her brows lifted in amusement.

Right.

Goals.

He cleared his throat, wishing he could clear the cloud of confusion that had swarmed through his brain. He stepped toward Christine and asked, "Would you like to dance?"

Christine had said no. Politely. Firmly. Then, with a small apologetic smile directed at Violet, she had glided away.

Was it obvious that Violet had developed feelings for the man she was supposed to be helping?

She'd really messed up his chances now.

"That didn't go very well." She stared after Christine. "I shouldn't have come."

"Of course you should. She knows we're just friends."

"Why do you keep pursuing her, anyway? You don't have that flicker and spark of something rare that I see with others. Like Dak and Miranda. Or Daisy-Mae and Maverick."

Her friend was in deep with Maverick. So deep. She just hoped he loved Daisy-Mae back in the same way.

Leo was blinking at her after that outburst.

She sighed. "Right. You don't need love because you don't fall. Sorry, carry on."

"I hit three things," Leo stated.

"Hmm?"

"It's second nature now. *Words.* I complimented her. I offered to lessen her burden and get her a drink. And then I also offered to spend quality time together with a dance."

"She's not a checklist, Leo. *Love* is not a checklist!" Violet whirled on him, suddenly angry. Angry for the way her heart was leading her on. Angry for the way she was falling for a man who was looking elsewhere. Angry for the way she kept having stupid moments with him where it felt like he might have an inkling of similar feelings for her.

But it just wasn't going to happen. And that made her angry, too.

"I thought I was doing well."

"We want *genuine*."

"I'm not?"

"Why do you want to be with Christine? What do you like about her as a person?"

Leo licked his lips and dropped his hands on his hips. His Adam's apple bobbed.

"Does she make you laugh? Can you imagine bringing her home to your family? Do you want to do the same things she does on days off? Or is it all one big business plan where you don't even care if you two can tolerate sharing the same space?"

Leo's shoulders had sagged and Violet felt like she'd just rained on his future parade.

"I'm sorry. That was really harsh."

"No, I appreciate the honesty. And truthfully, I don't know why I want this anymore."

They stared at each other for a long moment, Leo looking more and more dejected by the second.

"Come with me," she commanded, grabbing his

arm and dragging him toward the ballroom doors. There was a tall table by a white-and-gold-decorated Christmas tree and the CEO of Family Zone sat alone, nursing a drink, his earlier posse gone.

Perfect.

She stopped in front of the table. "Mr. Mc-Gregor, have you met Leo Pattra? He's one of the Dragons' newest players. "

"Yes, I'm familiar."

"As a former bull riding champion, he's worked with some high-profile companies in sponsorship agreements. I thought you might like to meet him before he gets swooped up, because he literally never stops talking about Family Zone and I think you'd be a great fit."

Leo reached forward, shaking hands. "Pleasure to meet you, Mr. McGregor."

"I believe your agent has contacted me a time or two."

"Leo is dogged when it comes to something he wants. He has some pretty thick blinders," Violet said, her tone dry.

Mr. McGregor chuckled. "Well, then that's something we have in common. Why don't you pull up a seat, if you can find one."

Leo quickly spun, finding a chair abandoned

by the wall. He placed it for Violet, then took her hand and helped her onto it.

She should have made herself scarce. The man was going to spend his few precious minutes with the CEO searching for a second chair for himself.

"He's quite the gentleman," Violet said, hoping to fill the awkward silence between herself and Mr. McGregor.

"You're his girlfriend?" Mr. McGregor asked. "Or are you a new agent?"

"Friend. And, um, I'm actually the team's mascot. I didn't want to come alone, and had nothing to wear and so Leo said…" She'd run a hand over the skirt of her dress, realizing she could easily make Leo sound like some sort of opportunistic sugar daddy rather than the generous and sweet friend that he was. "He's a very good friend. You'll find him to be loyal and kind."

Mr. McGregor studied her for a long moment and she wondered if he could tell that she was crushing on her friend. She could feel the heat in her face from not only speaking to him so confidently but also for complimenting Leo so blatantly.

"Well," Mr. McGregor said, "it sounds as though you're cut from the same cloth. He's lucky to have *you* as a friend."

Violet nodded, wishing the word *girl* was in front of that last word.

"You found one," she said, as Leo set a tall chair beside her. Mr. McGregor was sipping his drink, watching them. Leo gently touched her back, checking in with her."Did you want a drink?" he asked.

"No, thank you." Violet tipped her head toward the CEO, trying to mentally message that Leo should make his case quickly. She could sense Leo's nerves amplifying as he settled in his chair.

"So, what did you want to talk to me about?" Mr. McGregor asked, focusing his pale gray eyes on Leo. The man's voice was kind, but his demeanor meant business.

"I would like to work with you," Leo answered. "I am a clean-living man. I have experience filming commercials and representing a brand."

"He's convinced the Dragons' charity team that they need to take all the sick kids to a Family Zone theme park once they're well enough because he loves it so much and thinks they will too." She looked at Leo meaningfully.

He chuckled and gave her a grateful smile that turned sheepish as he faced Mr. McGregor.

"I think Family Zone is the best place ever. Whether you're a kid or an adult, there's something for everyone. And I think it would be amazing for the team to be able to send kids and their family there when they're feeling up to it."

"It would."

"I grew up on a ranch, and while we had a lot in many ways, we didn't have much for vacations. When I was thirteen, somehow my parents scraped enough together for all of us to go to Family Zone. Honestly, we were in danger of losing the ranch and I think they wanted to build some good family memories before things got hard."

Violet gave Leo's hand a squeeze as he blinked back emotion. He inhaled slowly and audibly, but the fine lines of pain still carved through his cheeks and forehead. That pain was still there, still fresh.

"Leo gave up college scholarships to help his family save the ranch once he was out of high school," she said quietly, hoping she wasn't overstepping by revealing this. But she could see how Mr. McGregor was reacting to Leo's story, and it was good.

Leo nodded.

"It sounds like your trip means a lot to you," the man said diplomatically.

"It's the only family vacation I can remember us taking together."

"Family Zone is a special place," Violet stated.

"It's somewhere families can create special memories that never fade. I want to share that with more people. Especially families who are going through a tough time. I know many people feel your theme parks are just fun and entertainment, but they're more than that. I'd love to work with your company in any way that you feel would be beneficial to you. I don't have a family of my own yet, but as you'll see by looking into my reputation with pro rodeo, I am steady and down to earth. I feel I'm suitable as a representative for your brand. I was a good representative for my sponsors and I can give you references, sir." Leo stood. "I would love to work with your company if you can find a place for me."

Mr. McGregor gestured for him to sit down again, then remained quiet for a long moment, while Violet held her breath.

"Tell your agent to call me on Monday. Actually, make it Tuesday. I need to talk to my team to see what we can find for a guy like you. I came here to check out the possibility of a hockey player representing us, unsure what that might look like. But talking to you tonight… Well, I'm getting an idea." He stood, reaching out to shake Leo's hand again. "I appreciate you sharing your story with me."

"Thank you, sir. I appreciate your time."

"And Leo?" Mr. McGregor sighed as though reluctant to do something. He fished around inside his jacket's inner pocket. "Any chance you could make a dad look like a hero to his sixteen-year-old daughter who's crazy about rodeo?" The man slid a postcard-sized image and marker across the table, and Leo gave a chuckle as he recognized the image of him astride a bucking Brahman bull.

"Want me to sign it?"

Mr. McGregor nodded and mentioned his daughter's name.

"I remember this." Leo waved the card and said to Violet, "I won one of the bigger belt buckles that day."

"My daughter watched all of your events. A big fan. Obviously, she made me bring this in case I saw you tonight." The older man pocketed the signed card. "Thank you."

"And thank you, sir."

Leo stepped away from the table, his palm on

Violet's lower back. He swiftly steered her through the large, beautifully decorated room, across the dance floor, through throngs of gossipers and out the exit at the opposite end of the room from where Mr. McGregor had been sitting.

Once out in the hallway, Leo let out a whoop and jumped into the air, punching the sky with a triumphant fist. "Did you see that?" he bellowed. "Did you hear what he said?"

Violet laughed. Leo was behaving like a wild man.

Or a man who'd just had a dream come true.

"You!" Leo stopped dancing and looked at her, his expression more joyful than she'd ever seen it. "You!" He came tearing across the red carpet and pulled her into a bear hug that lifted her from her feet. Laughing, he spun her in a circle, and she couldn't help but join in.

"You are the best thing that ever happened to me, Violet Granger." And then he planted a giant, happy kiss on her lips.

CHAPTER 8

*T*he game was not going well for the Dragons. Leo found himself becoming more and more distracted, doubting why he was here and why he'd even chosen hockey. The effort he'd poured into his skills on the ice wasn't making the impact he'd hoped for. It wasn't like rodeo, where he was just one athlete needing a turnaround. With a few right moves he could improve his stats in the ring and rise to the top again. Being on a struggling team was different, and it was frustrating.

At least he was now in talks with Family Zone, thanks to Violet. They were agonizingly slow, but the fact that they were even happening gave him hope that he'd be able to meet his financial dreams sooner rather than later.

It had been a month since the gala and Violet had been slightly standoffish since he'd kissed her without thinking. He'd been overjoyed and had crossed a line, and now it was impacting their friendship.

It was killing him, knowing she was upset with him.

He liked her and needed her in his life. Way more than Christine, who he hadn't seen nor missed since the gala.

But his friend Violet? He needed her. Life felt so…boring without her.

And he didn't know what to do, or how she was feeling. They'd been busy with Christmas, New Year's, engagement parties and games since the kiss. It felt like all they did was wave to each other from across rooms, and now they were reaching the end of January and still hadn't talked about it.

Maybe there was nothing to talk about. She'd given a nervous laugh after he'd laid his lips on hers, and had brushed it off, her face red.

And yet things hadn't been the same since.

The ref's whistle blew, and as players rearranged themselves for a face-off, men slipped on and off the bench around Leo. The team. This game. They'd started their season as the worst-rated not just in their division but in the entire league. They'd made some strides and were no longer at the bottom of the pack, but the fans were getting annoyed by their lack of wins.

So was he. So was the team.

He could feel the energy coming off the men on the bench beside him. Dejection. Maybe a touch of despair. And the crowd behind their box was rapidly sliding from frustration into annoyance with the widening point gap. There were only five minutes left in the game, and a win would need a miracle.

Maverick came off the ice, jammed himself into the tight spot between Leo and Mullens, pulled off his helmet and squirted water over his sweat-soaked head.

Leo noticed that within a few seconds his eyes drifted to the stands, which was unlike the captain, who normally maintained a steadfast focus on the game. Did he feel the shift in energy as well?

Leo found his own gaze rising to the stands.

Not too far to his right he spotted Violet in the Dezzie costume, and Daisy-Mae dancing beside her. They were working hard to get the audience behind the players' box excited, to shift the energy momentum into something more positive. Kids near them cheered and took part, the adults not so much.

Leo looked away, uncomfortable about the way he'd kissed Violet without thinking about how she'd feel about it. There'd been moments of attraction between them, but he must have read it wrong because now he was facing losing his friend.

He knew nothing about romance, that was for sure. A "moment" didn't mean a woman wanted a kiss.

He rubbed his lips, practically tasting her peach-flavored lip gloss despite the time and distance from that quick smooch. Man, if he was going to ruin things with her, couldn't he have at least given her a hint of how he could really kiss instead of that bruising quick one?

He sighed, his attention drifting back to the stands. Dezzie was moving closer to the team's players box, high-fiving some fans wearing straw cowboy hats with the Dragons logo on the front. From what he'd heard, Daisy-Mae, as part of her additional full-time job in the head office, had arranged for them to be given out at home games.

It was nice to see people wearing their gear. Now they just had to win more to keep those fans. Because it was a simple equation: no fans, no hockey.

No hockey, no Violet.

No hockey, no money. No retirement plan. No security.

Leo jiggled his legs, his chest tight, his gloves abandoned at his feet, no longer expecting to be sent into the game at a second's notice. He pushed the tips of his fingers into the knitted hockey socks that came up over his knees, trying to ground himself. The woven material had ridges and valleys, perfectly sized for his fingertips.

They were still down on the scoreboard.

He glanced behind him.

Dezzie was still dancing.

Violet was normally so positive, so optimistic in the way she thought and spoke that Leo didn't want to think how she might be feeling inside her costume right now. He hoped the fans weren't yelling at her. She deserved better. And not just from spectators, but from guys who called themselves her friends.

"Eyes on the ice," the coach snapped.

"Yes, sir," Leo said. Maverick shot him a guilty

look, and they both turned their attention back to the game.

The team captain sure had it bad for Daisy-Mae. Leo smirked at him and got a scowl in return. Women. So distracting.

The other team scored a goal and the tension on the bench increased, as well as in the stands. Leo could feel it down his back, an unpleasant prickling sensation. It spread up his spine, through to the base of his skull, then over his scalp like it was covered in ants.

When he felt like this in a rodeo, something bad was going to happen.

He jiggled his legs again, feeling claustrophobic in the players' box.

Another face-off. The Dragons lost it, the opposing team in possession of the puck and already racing over the blue line, lining up for the shot.

Moments later, angry shouts erupted behind the bench in spite of Landon's great save. Despite Coach Louis's earlier reprimand, Leo turned. A fan in a Dragons jersey was squaring off with Dezzie, arms waving, face red.

Leo stood.

"Sit down," the coach growled.

"You're facing the wrong way, Socks," Maverick said mildly, before swinging himself over the boards and onto the rink, back on the ice to try and save the game.

Leo scanned the stands for security guards. None. He looked at the guards normally seated near their box to protect the players. They hadn't heard the shouts, and he was unable to make eye contact with them.

The man several rows above the box shoved Dezzie, sending her tumbling into Daisy-Mae, who'd been trying to talk reason into him.

Leo unlatched the gate that kept fans from entering the players' area. He was over barricades and empty seats before anyone had a chance to grab him, before he had a chance to think. His skate blades clanked against the concrete steps as he closed the distance between himself and Violet.

Other fans had circled the fallen mascot in shock, but because of the staggered seats, few could get to the angry man, who was about to reach down and shake her.

Leo leaped up the final three steps and grabbed the guy in a bear hug. He fisted the back hem of the man's Dragons jersey, and in one fluid move, yanked it up over the man's head in a familiar hockey-fight move, restricting the assailant's arms as well as impairing his ability to see.

In a flash, two security guards flanked the fan as Leo pulled back his fist.

"No," Daisy-Mae warned, and he caught himself before he completed the swing, adrenaline surging through him.

Daisy-Mae, who'd tumbled after Dezzie collided with her, was back on her feet, pulling on Violet's dragon costume head, which had gotten wedged between two rows of seats, trapping Violet. As soon as it was free, Leo grabbed Violet's arm like he had on the day they'd met, hoisting her to her feet. He clasped her headpiece, angling it downward so he could peer through the shaded eyeholes.

"Are you okay?" he asked, his heart screaming like he'd just raced a bull across the ring, climbing the fence at the last possible moment before the beast crashed into it with its horns.

He could barely see Violet's face inside.

"She says she's fine," Daisy-Mae said quietly.

How could she be? She'd just been shouted at and shoved, wedged into a vulnerable position. If she'd needed to, she couldn't have escaped or defended herself.

He saw a glimmer through the eyeholes. A tear. Wetness on her cheek.

Leo's hands tightened back into fists and he whirled, searching for the tough guy in the jersey. He was being marched away by security, and Leo's desire to chase them down and pummel him intensified. He leaned forward to pursue him up the steps, but more security guards had filled the small area, blocking him. He swore under his breath and ushered Violet into the ring of safety they created.

"Don't let her come back out again tonight," he ordered, and Daisy-Mae nodded briskly, her face pale.

"You better get back on the ice," someone said, firmly pushing the thick padding of his equipment, directing him away from the scene, the stands and Violet.

She was moving up the stairs to the next level, waving and blowing kisses as if nothing had happened. But inside the dragon costume, Leo knew she was crying.

And it was the worst feeling in the world.

* * *

Violet didn't know if the team had won or lost. But she guessed that unless a miracle had occurred, the game was not only over, but the Dragons had endured another big loss.

She sat on the bench in her changing room, unable to pull herself together enough to leave. Nobody out there would be spitting on her, squaring up to her or challenging her, like they had when she was in costume. She'd be an anonymous employee in street clothes, wearing an ID badge.

Still, she couldn't force her legs to lift her from the bench, to move toward the door.

While in costume she knew enough to avoid the area behind the opposing team's box. Knew to avoid the aggressive calls that would draw her over, the type of spectator who would try to spit on her or trip her. But behind her own team? That had taken her by surprise.

"Security said they'll walk us out when you're ready," Daisy-Mae said. She'd locked the door as soon as they'd been deposited there by the guards. She'd helped Violet out of her costume with shaking hands and a pale face, voicing a stream of apologies for not being a better lookout.

Violet wasn't ready to leave the room or even

process what had happened. She felt like she was going to vomit. Or run.

Courage. She drew a deep breath and stood.

"Do you think Leo will get in trouble?" she asked.

Daisy-Mae shook her head, then shrugged.

He'd busted right out of the players' box and raced up the stands to protect her during the game.

Who did that?

And what did it mean?

A million thoughts swarmed her brain, from how the press was going to portray him as a crazy hothead, to whether Family Zone would drop him, to the kiss he'd given her at the gala.

She hadn't told Daisy-Mae about that because she feared her friend would read too much into it. He'd been excited, and the kiss had meant nothing.

She wanted it to, though. But she was also wise enough to know he was looking for something different, despite them being great together as friends.

Violet sank down on the locker room bench again, needing another minute before facing the outside world.

"That was pretty sexy, him running up to help

you like that," Daisy-Mae commented. She'd figured out Violet was crushing even though she didn't know the full extent of it.

"Yeah."

"How are you feeling?"

"Shaky." Violet held up her hands, which were trembling.

"That was really scary, Vi. I'm so—"

"You don't need to apologize again. I felt the shift in the crowd and ignored it, too. I thought I could change their mood. We've done it before."

"I'm the one not hidden inside a big costume. I should have pulled you out of the stands earlier. And of course you're shaky. You were attacked! That's not supposed to happen. Ever."

Violet nodded, knowing the unexpected aggression aimed at her wasn't the only reason she was shaky. She'd been shocked, sure, but Dezzie's thick, soft exterior had protected her from any physical harm. That and Leo's timely arrival.

Her tears of surprise, shock and fear had quickly dried, the threatened feeling overshadowed by several facts. One, Leo had noticed her in the stands. And not somewhere easy, like across the rink, where he might glance up from the game and see her. She had been *behind* him. Two, despite being locked into the players' box, he'd done something about the aggressive fan. *Him*. Not security or anyone else. He'd broken past barriers, skates and all, to rip the man off her. And then he'd looked through her costume's eyeholes and seen her. He'd *seen* her.

And he'd been livid. He'd been so scared that she was hurt.

How could she not turn those things into a familiar story she loved—the one where the man she liked was crushing right back at her?

Daisy-Mae was asking her something.

"Do you want to make a break for it?"

Violet focused on the here and now. There were voices in the hall. The postgame hoop-la must be over, the word about what had happened spreading. The entire team must now be aware of what Leo had done, and there was no way she could face them all, leaving at the same time. The sympathy, the questioning looks… Too much.

There was a knock on the door, and Violet quickly dabbed at her cheeks, where tears had streaked anew. Daisy-Mae unlocked the door and peeked through the gap. She opened it wider and Violet stood up, unsure what to expect. Was she going to get in trouble from Nuvella for some reason? Was the press going to track her down and demand information about the attack, serving up her hurt for the world to devour as entertainment?

Leo appeared in the doorway, his hair damp, dripping onto the collar of his white shirt, which was only partially buttoned, the cuffs loose, his suit jacket bunched in his right hand. He quickly scanned the room, latching on to her with his gaze. She raised a hand to her forehead, sheltering her red, puffy eyes from his view. Suddenly she was engulfed in a warm, soap-scented hug, his arms wrapped tightly around her, his bag and jacket landing at her feet.

A sob escaped her chest, and she shuddered in his embrace as she tried to draw a breath.

"It's okay. I'm here. You're safe." His palm stroked the back of her head, calming her, as his other one rubbed her back. His hands were warm, the feel of his firm, solid body soothing and safe.

She heard the door thump shut as Daisy-Mae left.

As Violet settled, Leo eased his grip, craning his neck to peer down at her. He'd felt like a warm, cozy comforter after a long, hard day, and she longed for him to continue the hug.

"Are you all right?" He was studying her, checking for injuries, his right hand gently cupping her face so he could take a better look. "Are you hurt anywhere?"

Tears returned as she shook her head. "I'm okay." She stepped from his arms, tugging down the sleeves of her sweatshirt so they covered her hands. "Although I'm probably getting fired."

"Are you kidding me?" He looked livid again, like he wanted to kick something. "I hope they fine that guy for assault."

Her tears dried, and she gaped at him.

"Don't look at me like that. He pushed you down!" Leo's hands had bunched into fists, and he shoved his unbuttoned shirtsleeves up, revealing the cords of muscles in his forearms.

He seemed ready to fight. That same fierce look was blazing in his eyes, like it had in the stands. As if he was ready to kill for her.

It took her breath away.

"Did you get in trouble?" she asked, realizing that him racing up the stands in his skates and manhandling a fan was probably against a dozen rules and could get him benched or fined.

"Coach muttered something about letting security handle stuff in the future." Leo squeezed his eyes shut for a brief second, the fight leaving him. "Do you think this'll impact things with Family Zone?" He shook his head and opened them again, that fight blazing back. "I don't care."

"Leo!"

"No." He inhaled unsteadily and faced her. "What would have happened if I hadn't got up there when I did?"

"There was security."

"Too little, too late. I'll take the consequences, because you matter more to me than any deal ever could."

* * *

Leo couldn't stop thinking about yesterday's game and how Violet had been pushed down by that fan. The media was in a frenzy over it, and she was refusing to talk about it with anyone. He'd been interviewed—well, there had been requests, but Nuvella, Louis and Miranda had handled his statements and talked to the press on his behalf.

"Are you sure the parade is a good idea?" Leo glanced at the rows of floats waiting to roll down Sweetheart Creek's Main Street, tossing candy and advertising local businesses for the first annual Armadillo Day. The idea, from what he'd gathered, was that the day had involved some events and games along Main Street, with money being raised to take care of repairing the town's outdoor swimming pool. Donations were also being taken for a local animal shelter, which was being built by Brant Wylder, the town's veterinarian.

Leo hadn't made it to the pancake breakfast or any of the afternoon events, but was here for the evening parade, which would kick off the food trucks, dance and fireworks.

Violet had somehow wrangled him into joining the parade, along with herself, dressed as Dezzie. Naturally, Daisy-Mae was also coming, to ensure that Violet didn't get run over by a decorated tractor.

Currently, Daisy-Mae was off to the side, chatting with someone, while Violet stood in her dragon costume with the head tucked under her arm, flouting the head-always-on-in-public rule. Then again, there weren't any dressing rooms on the field, so she could argue that the staging grounds were her locker room.

It was already dark out, the parade preparations illuminated by the football field's lights. Daisy-Mae had outfitted Leo with one of the Dragons' cowboy hats, which she'd studded with small blinking lights. Being a night parade, everything that could be lit up was. One guy who'd walked by even had twinkling cowboy boots.

"Don't forget to make yourself accessible for photographs." Violet pointed into her dragon head and Leo reached inside for a stack of hockey cards. He glanced at them, surprised to see they were of him. He was on a card! His number, with a candid shot of him skating. Looking comfortable on skates, just like a pro hockey player.

"Whoa."

"Nice photo, right?"

"Where'd you get these?"

"Daisy-Mae snuck them out of Nuvella's office. Technically, they aren't available yet, so mum's the word."

"Are we going to get in trouble for handing them out?"

"Probably."

He chuckled. Violet's rebellious side still surprised him sometimes. Less so than when he'd first met her, as he was getting used to seeing her spunkiness.

"What do you say when someone asks for a selfie with you?" she prompted.

"Say cheese?"

"Say 'be sure to tag me and the Dragons if you post this on social media.'"

"Right." She had a lot of rules about the parade and how he was to act. He appreciated it, though. She was making sure he benefited from tonight in terms of visibility and image.

"Try to get photos with kids in them. Family Zone will love that."

"Reputation enhancement," he muttered. That's what Nuvella called it.

The media was divided about the way he'd stormed the stands to protect Violet. They'd loved that he was loyal and protective, looking out for the team's mascot. But he could see how quickly and easily he could be painted as an uncontrollable hothead who roughed up fans.

Not that he'd roughed up the man.

But he'd wanted to.

The only saving grace was that he wasn't a big fighter on the ice and didn't have any prior hothead moments for them to build a reputation off of. Honestly, he was still too focused on the puck and getting to it before anyone else that he didn't even consider decking an opponent or slamming them into the boards.

As long as nothing else happened, the whole incident could hopefully be forgotten.

"Do you think the town will have any issue

with me being in the parade? You know—the hot-head fighter rep that's trying to stick to me?"

"Are you kidding?" Her expression was almost tender. "They think you're a hero. They all know who's inside Dezzie."

He felt a weight lift off him, knowing there were some folks on his side. Folks whose respect he wanted to earn.

The floats lined up in front of them started crawling toward the exit from the football field staging grounds, and Leo hoped that the favors Violet had asked from Daisy-Mae would pay off for himself and the team.

"And if anyone mentions football, smile and wave and say 'Go Torpedos!'" she coached.

"Right. Town's team. Got it. Football all the way." He glanced down at his Dragons jersey. Hopefully there were a few hockey fans watching the parade tonight.

Daisy-Mae hustled up and slid Violet's earpiece into place, then disappeared again. No doubt, helping their friend Jenny with some finishing touches on her boutique's float.

"And don't let me get run over!" Violet added. She tilted her head toward the tractor behind them. It was lit up with spinning lights and advertised cattle feed.

"Wait," Leo said, feeling panicked. "Didn't you say there was some guy in town who drove his tractor when he was under the influence, in hopes of avoiding a ticket?" Was this old guy him? He seemed sober. A bit ancient, but sober.

"You'll be fine."

Leo picked up his pace, putting more distance between himself and the trailing tractor, hoping the parade didn't end his career—or his life. He was wearing what he thought of as his lucky belt buckle tonight, but wasn't sure if it would protect him from a tractor driver nodding off and flattening him by accident.

Violet flashed him a smile and lifted her dragon head, about to put it on. A swell of gratitude washed over him for the good friend she was, and the way things were going back to normal between them again.

"Vi!" He hurried to her side and she paused. "Everyone needs a friend like you. And I don't know how to thank you for all of this. The connections you helped me make at the gala, and then this event, too."

She shrugged. "Sometimes all you need is a good friend."

"You're getting me to all the places I want to be. And I appreciate it."

She bobbed her head. "I know."

"So, thanks." He shifted awkwardly, wanting to say more. He wanted to tell her he was over Christine, and that the whole idea of *marrying* her had been a dumb one. It was embarrassing how long it had taken him to understand that Christine Lagrée wasn't into him and never would be. If he had time later, he wanted to tell Violet about his parents' anniversary party and how his previous view on marriage had been all wrong. She'd been right about so many things—naturally, as she was the one with experience when it came to falling in love.

"Parade in less than one minute. Positions now, everyone, or I'll have you and your float removed!" Henry Wylder snapped through a megaphone, walking the line of floats.

Violet gave Leo a wry look, suppressing her giggles at Henry's crankiness. Leo shook his head and sighed. This town.

He squeezed Violet's arm through the costume padding. "Anyway, I just wanted to say thank you."

"Of course."

"And also, I'm sorry if I overstepped."

She gave him a blank look.

"Get in position with the dragon, Daisy-Mae!" Henry ordered.

"At the gala," Leo explained. "I crossed our friendship line, and I'm sorry."

Violet gave him a steady look. "I'm not." Then she dropped the dragon head over her own, masking her expression.

What?

She wasn't sorry he'd kissed her?

Wait. Were they even talking about the same thing?

But if she wasn't sorry about the kiss, then why had she acted so weird for weeks?

Maybe it had been about something else?

Either way, if she wasn't sorry about the kiss, then most definitely, neither was he.

CHAPTER 9

"You look exhausted," Violet said through her microphone to Daisy-Mae, as the parade began moving toward the street to start its route through town.

She needed to distract herself, release that dizzy feeling that was making her light-headed.

I'm not.

I'm not sorry you kissed me, Leo. I only wished it had meant something big to you, that I was the kind of woman you were looking for.

Yeah, she needed a worthy distraction, and focusing on her friend's exhaustion was a good place to start.

"Mav and I've been busy. Especially since the engagement and interviews and such. Everything's crazy, you know? It's just a lot of press and scheduling and time apart."

"You doing okay, though?"

There was something in her friend's voice that suggested things were far from okay with her and Maverick. The two had started out as friends, fake dating in an attempt to fix his reputation. Then suddenly the whole fake relationship thing went prime time, with public grand gestures. Violet was best friends with Daisy-Mae and even she wasn't sure what was real and what wasn't anymore.

"Yeah, of course. We're fine," Daisy-Mae said quickly. "I couldn't help but notice that you seem more yourself again lately."

"Me?" She knew her friend was trying to change the subject, but her statement was too intriguing to ignore.

"I'm glad you're having fun again. Especially today."

She felt the familiar, unpleasant tug in her gut when she thought about her failed wedding. Today would have been her third wedding anniversary. Long enough that it was time to fully let it go—something she felt like she was finally succeeding at.

"Of course I am," she said. "Let's hear it for Armadillo Day!"

"Did you see the giant paper mâché statue of Bill?" Daisy-Mae said with a laugh.

She had. Bill, the town's wild and cranky armadillo had become a bit of a mascot for Sweetheart Creek, and a local artist had recreated the creature at about twenty times life size for one float. It was hideous, and she loved it dearly.

"Who doesn't love a huge armadillo?" she asked, giggling. She'd bought the Bill T-shirt and ball cap that Brant and April were selling to raise funds for the new animal shelter they were building. "Life is for living, right?"

"It sure is. And it always helps to move on with a tasty crush?"

Violet groaned at Daisy-Mae's hinting tone. "There are no tasty crushes happening. And lower your voice. You know how easily rumors start around here." Plus, Leo was only a few feet away from Daisy-Mae and might overhear.

"Well, whatever's going on, I remember how last year on the anniversary of you and Wyatt..." Daisy-Mae let her voice trail off.

Right. Last year she'd been crying into a drink at the Watering Hole with April and Daisy-Mae, her usual sunny it's-okay attitude irretrievable for a full eighteen hours while she'd wallowed.

Sure, she'd decided to stay in town and had found a beautiful home, the friends she'd made sticking by her side, but she'd still held so much anger. Why couldn't Wyatt have expressed his doubts instead of making such a fool out of her in front of everyone? Why had he stolen their day like that? It was supposed to be *their* moment. It was the event she'd longed for since she was a kid.

Yet she also knew her ex had done her a tremendous favor by running out of that church. Most days she thought she'd forgiven him and moved on, his leaving her stunned and heartbroken at the altar no longer her first thought in the morning when she woke up. But some days it still caught up with her, knocked her down at the knees, reminding her what a failure she was when it came to love, and how that dang curse flowed through the generations with unrelenting determination.

Well, it wouldn't get her down any longer. Not worth it. She was out searching for love, putting bandage after bandage over her broken heart.

Each day was better and soon she'd be fully healed, if that was truly a possibility. And sure, it likely wouldn't be today, as it was filled with too many memories not to cause some bumps.

"So what's going on?" Daisy-Mae prompted.

Oh, man. She'd been incredibly foolish telling Leo she hadn't minded their kiss. Just because he didn't seem to be actively pursuing Christine any longer didn't mean he was ready for true love and a happily ever after with her.

"Nothing."

"Don't play innocent. I know that tone."

"There's no tone."

Telling Daisy-Mae would make things messy. Her friend would either try to help or she'd be full of warnings about how busy hockey players were, and how the media could swarm the two of you and ruin it all.

Case in point, Leo had endured a lot of speculation and fuss over him rescuing her—even though nobody knew she had been the one inside the costume. If they started dating and people found out he'd gone all hotheaded to protect *her*...

Well, she probably wouldn't be the only weak-kneed woman in the state of Texas.

"You were talking to Leo," Daisy-Mae prompted.

"Yup."

"You organized this for him."

"Yup."

"You're trying to help him like I'm helping Maverick with his image."

"That's going well, isn't it?" The parade was moving forward, Leo off to one side, thumbing through the player cards she'd given him. "He's getting attention from brands and stuff, right?"

"So? Are you going to ask him out?" Daisy-Mae pressed.

"What? Leo? *No*. Not his type."

"You have a chance to find love, Vi. You can't give up."

"I'm not giving up."

"Do I need to start clucking like a chicken? Because you like him."

"Daise! I've put myself out there for so many men who just weren't feeling it the way I was. I was blind and stupid and hurt myself. I can see he's not into me like that, so there is no way I'm doing anything about my crush. Not this time."

"So you are crushing."

"I'm also on a dating app, being selective, and most importantly, looking for men who *want* someone like me, as well as marriage and love. And they want it soon. Not in ten years."

"You're on a dating app?"

"Yes."

She'd initially taken the step to ensure she didn't sit at home and brood over the man she couldn't have. So far, she'd narrowed her selection to a few nice guys, and they were messaging regularly through the app. Next week, in a brave moment, she planned to ask each of her top picks out for coffee to meet them in real life.

"I'm sorry I haven't been around for Dragon Babes more," Daisy-Mae said.

"It's fine." Violet sighed.

"Really, I am. I feel bad."

"For working hard to connect with the love of your life? Don't be sorry. I'm just being a mope because I keep falling for men who aren't into me."

"It's okay to mope."

"I hear men find that very attractive."

Daisy-Mae choked on a laugh. "I've missed you." Violet felt her friend hug her side through the thick costume.

"I've missed you, too."

"You deserve to find awesome love at its finest, Vi. You've worked so hard and been hurt so bad. You're tough."

Violet's eyes welled up. "I don't feel tough. Half the time I wonder what's the point of it all?"

"Of what?" Daisy-Mae's voice had grown cautious.

"Dating and trying? Love? The hope of finding it? Why do I still want it when all it's done is destroy me?" She held in a sob, the hurt forming a lump in her chest. She was crying in her costume again. In her periphery, she saw Leo turn to face her for a second, as though sensing it.

Leo. She wanted Leo. To make things worse for her heart, she'd heard rumors of trade talks happening between the Dragons and another team thousands of miles away.

Leo was being considered.

Her friend might leave.

Why was she the one stuck behind every time?

"Stupid curse," she muttered, momentarily forgetting that her headset picked up every sound, relaying it to Daisy-Mae.

"You're tougher and more determined than some weary old curse that's got to be wearing off by now," her friend replied with a tone of authority. "And besides, think of how many potentially horrible love-match dudes it's already removed from your life."

Violet groaned, not wanting to consider it.

"Lots, right? Which means it's got to be losing

its strength. I mean, you didn't even get past flirting with Owen."

Violet perked up. "Assuming curses are real, and I'm not actually using the idea as a crutch to excuse my own shortcomings or to hold me back, could a curse actually lose strength? Could you break them without knowing?"

"Of course!"

"But with Owen leaving before we started dating, wouldn't that suggest the curse is getting stronger, since he left before we fell in love?"

"No, not at all. The curse would have let you both fall in love, and *then* he would have gone back to baseball. Anyway, I believe the next guy's gonna stick. You're going to find so much stinking love with him that it blasts the curse all the way back to the grave of the cranky old biddy who summoned bad juju on your great-gran."

"Bad juju is no match for me or the love I'm going to find," Violet said, testing the idea out loud. "That dating app isn't going to know what hit it come tomorrow morning, when I start mes-saging all those potential matches!"

"That's the spirit."

"This'll be fun!"

With a bounce in her step, Violet reached the

street, waving to people sitting in lawn chairs along the sidewalks and curbs.

"This kid over here wants a hug, Dezzie."

Violet followed Daisy-Mae to the edge of the street. A small body hugged her leg, and she patted the child's back, then did a few dance moves.

"Next fall, if I haven't found love yet," Violet vowed as they moved on, "I'm getting Jackie to take me to some football games."

"Matchmaker magic!" Daisy-Mae sang as they continued on. "That's right, baby!"

"Matched up, married off."

"In the meantime you could tell a certain someone you like him and see what happens. He might be closer than you think when it comes to being on the same page about relationships."

"He isn't."

"Have you asked him?"

"It's pretty much all we've discussed lately."

"Oh! There's Mrs. Fisher! Blow her a kiss!"

Daisy-Mae moved gracefully under the street-lights, people swaying with glow sticks as she passed. She looked like a beauty queen in her jersey and hat. Smiling, waving in the January night, moving with the floats.

Violet wanted to be like her when she grew

up. Sort of like a modern-day fairy tale, where curses held no power over her.

Actually, a lot like how she'd felt the night of the gala when she'd been Leo's date. She'd felt like a beautiful, powerful princess. Leo had been such a great support, sending her off to buy a gorgeous dress, setting her up with a makeover that had given her confidence to help him land Family Zone.

As the parade continued toward Main Street, Violet mulled over the idea of telling him how she felt. Try as she might, she just couldn't see how they would fit together with their different views and wants when it came to love.

The obvious pro to telling him would be that maybe he felt the same way and they might figure out a way to live happily ever after.

The con list was pretty long, though. She didn't want to wait until he had some giant sum of money stashed away before starting a family. She also wanted true love. That romantic, sweep-you-away kind of love, which hadn't made it onto Leo's must-have list. And while she felt flickers of something special between them, the kiss—platonic and spontaneous—had only made things weird. Point in fact, it had taken Leo over a month to even mention it.

Another con was that her telling Leo she liked him could potentially be the end of their friendship. And she needed him. He made her feel special, seen and understood. He was helping her regain her footing in life, get some spunk in her step. She didn't want to lose that. But the risk of it happening was still way too great.

* * *

By the time they reached the end of the parade route, Leo's cheeks hurt from smiling, and his hand was cramped from signing so many hockey cards. If anyone phoned him right now he was fairly confident he would answer, "And if you post this photo on social media, be sure to tag me and the Dragons!"

At least it had kept his mind busy, because Violet stating that she didn't regret him kissing her did not compute. Her actions didn't suggest she was cool with being kissed.

Despite his sore cheeks, he felt the beginnings of another smile. But what if she really *was* cool with it and that was why she'd acted weird?

The thought brought him to a full grin.

He was cool with kissing.

He'd lost sight of Violet and Daisy-Mae about

halfway down Main Street, falling far behind. He'd started near the beginning of the parade and ended near the back, and at one point had been walking with an older dog on a leash. Leo was pretty sure the man who'd given him the leash was the same Brant Wylder who'd named Violet's cat Onesie.

The dog had been amazing, patient and quiet, even posing for photos with its little vest that said Please Donate to the Future Sweetheart Creek Animal Shelter. The vest had a thoughtfully placed pocket for donations, which Leo had added to. By the time Brant retrieved the animal, Leo had told him if it ever needed a home to call him.

The man had tucked a business card in Leo's hand with a smile and a promise to phone him on Monday.

Did he even have time to take proper care of a pet, with his frequent travels? And how had that dog wormed its way into his heart so quickly, anyway?

As he passed the food trucks parked along a closed-to-traffic side street, he bought two ciders, certain Violet would be thirsty when he finally found her. Slipping back onto Main, nodding to people as he went, he thought he saw

Dezzie barrel into a store called Blue Tumbleweed. He had a feeling Violet couldn't wait to get out of her costume. Together, they'd driven into town from her house, and she'd slipped into her costume on the field. Did she need him to walk her back there to shed the costume and leave it in his car?

He entered the store, glancing around for a dragon. No sign.

He recognized Violet's friends April and Hannah, who'd been in the parade on different floats, pitching in to help customers.

Jenny, who he'd met at Thanksgiving, said to him from her spot at the cash register, "She's in the back performing her metamorphosis."

"What?"

"She's getting out of costume."

"Oh, right. Thanks." He set the hot paper cups on a nearby windowsill, then ducked behind a mannequin as some giggling women moved past outside. They'd already accosted him twice for selfies and had requested he give them autographs in places Family Zone wouldn't approve of.

"You hiding?"

Leo turned, to find teammate Dylan O'Neill standing there. The Dragons' center was out of his cast and due back on the ice as soon as his foot rehab was completed—several weeks, tops.

"Hey, what's up? Checking out the parade?"

Dylan shrugged and glanced upward. "Yeah, thought I'd pop by. Your cowboy hat's blinking."

"Oh." Leo reached up, removed it and turned off the lights, feeling guilty that Dylan hadn't been asked to join the parade, but had come out from the city to be a part of the festivities anyway. "You should have been in the parade, man."

"Nah, the foot."

"You could've walked that far." The town's population was barely over 4,000, and for a bit Leo had thought the parade might loop through it twice, just to seem bigger. Then again, Violet had put him in the parade as some sort of favor, not even inviting Maverick to join them—and he lived out here. Although, from what Leo gathered, Maverick was triple-booked these days and unlikely to be able to carve out time for something fun, like tonight. The guy's career was exploding, and Leo couldn't wait to see if his own did the same.

He heard a familiar voice across the store, then women whispering.

Jenny was pointing at Dylan, who was poking at a few of her displays. Western wear wasn't the man's style, but Leo figured he'd come for something other than a new shirt or buckle.

"Do me a favor and take him with you?" Jenny said to Violet.

She nodded and headed Leo's way.

"Hey. Are you hiding?" she asked him.

He was still hunched behind the mannequin, but promptly straightened, trying to stop himself from staring at her lips.

She hadn't minded the kiss. *The kiss.*

"There you are." He gave her arm a squeeze, then spun, lifting the cups of cider off the windowsill. "I thought you might be thirsty, and this was the only decaffeinated warm drink I could find from the food trucks."

"Thanks."

"I was going to get hot chocolate from one truck, but there was a hissing armadillo with a dish of spilled corn fritters threatening anyone who came near."

"Sounds like Bill's discovered Armadillo Day."

"This town is so odd."

"One of the many reasons I love it. Want to walk?" She headed for the door, and Leo nodded, following. She looked over her shoulder. "Dylan? You coming?"

"I think I want a pair of boots. You go ahead."

He lifted one nearby. It was pale blue with white stitching and a silver toe plate.

Leo snorted. The dude was so transparent. He obviously cared nothing about the night's parade and activities. "Those are women's boots," he muttered to Dylan as they left.

The man shrugged, set it down and picked up another one.

Violet was giggling by the time they hit the sidewalk. "An enemies-to-lovers story coming up for them in three, two, one…?"

"I can only laugh, thinking about how Jenny might react to the idea." The poor woman had looked exasperated just having Dylan in her store.

Leo and Violet moved along the street, the occasional person asking for a selfie or auto-graph. The cowboys, however, made eye contact and tipped their hats in a silent hello. He tipped his hat back, liking the town more and more with each block they walked. He felt like he fit in here.

"This place reminds me of Montana's cattle country."

They'd stopped walking and when Violet didn't answer, he followed her line of sight. Jenny's float was parked at the end of Main Street.

Even Leo could tell that it was the prettiest one, making promises of beauty and dreams.

The flatbed trailer had been covered with shaggy white carpet, and a rose-bedecked archway with small white lights. Bright silk flowers complimented the colored gowns and wedding finery displayed on mannequins, a signal to the town that Jenny was ready to set up prom-goers and anyone recently engaged.

Leo knew Violet could feel his gaze traveling along with hers, but she didn't bother to look away. She'd always been open about the hope that one day she'd be wearing one of those dresses with the long train and beaded bodice. He admired her strength, her conviction despite her bad luck.

"Tell me." He scooped her free hand into his, hoping she'd help him understand what a woman like her thought about love, and how he could find it for himself.

Violet tore her eyes away from the float's flowered archway. It was just waiting for a bride to stand under it and proclaim her love to the man who would soon become her husband. That one moment representing the beginning of something special, a sacred bond.

It all felt so terribly unfair.

She knew Daisy-Mae would get her way, her man, her wedding, her dream. Her friend would be cherished and loved. For always and forever.

But Violet herself? She wasn't feeling as certain as she had been forty minutes ago, during Daisy-Mae's pep talk.

"Vi?" Leo prompted softly.

"It's just…" How could she explain to someone who didn't believe he could fall in love?

"You like weddings? Hate them?" His voice lowered. "Bad memories?"

Yes to all the above.

And especially today.

"I'm just…conflicted. I still want this, and yeah, it hurts. Today was supposed to be…" Her voice broke, and she sighed.

Leo squeezed her hand. "You still want the whole package."

She nodded.

"I admire that."

She turned, searching through the crowds behind them, where entertainers and booths had been moved onto the street once the parade finished. She wasn't sure why she was thinking of

Daisy-Mae right now and how her friend was in the thick of it, figuring it out, struggling through the tough stuff around love.

Could Violet do that with Leo, or were they too different to ever find common ground when it came to a lasting relationship full of love?

And was the temptation to attempt that with him simply because she was feeling wounded, vulnerable and lonely tonight?

Now wasn't the time to try and solve this dilemma.

"You want a traditional wedding?" Leo asked.

"Yes," she said, feeling exasperated with his persistence in sticking to the topic. Everything to do with marriage and love was one step in the opposite direction from Leo, and she just wanted to enjoy the calm security of their friendship tonight.

"Yeah? Big or small?"

"Can we not do this right now?"

"Do what?"

"This." She waved her hand. Why had she told him she hadn't minded the kiss? Why?

"I'm curious, though. I want to understand and see it the way you do."

She stared at Jenny's float again, mentally choosing which dress she'd wear to her own wedding. What was the danger in telling him what she wanted? It might actually protect her, send him a step or two further away from her, widen that distance she so desperately needed in order to think straight tonight.

She faced him, voice firm. "I want biggish."

"Why's that?"

Her breath left her as the familiar image came to mind of what her wedding day would be like. Her walking down the aisle as the center of attention. Everyone standing to watch her pass. The little girls wanting to grow up to be like her.

"You'll never look as radiant and beautiful as you do on your wedding day. I want that day," she said firmly. "The whole, entire day. Not just the dress-up part. I want everyone in my life to celebrate with me. To celebrate love. I want the wedding to mark the beginning of an unbreakable bond I hope we'll always have. A husband and partner who'll be there even when his fears are striking at him. A man who'll be there with me through all of the changes life throws at us. Moving in together, having children, changing jobs, vacations, retirement, sickness, health, grandchildren. Everything. Shoulder to shoulder, through thick and thin."

"That sounds beautiful." Leo squeezed her hand again.

She gently extracted it from his. His gaze was filled with genuine caring, and she knew she trusted him implicitly. Maybe even more than she'd ever trusted Wyatt. Leo was filling so many holes in her life, holes she hadn't even realized existed.

But he was just a friend. An important friend.

She turned away, afraid that her true feelings, which had been growing stronger and stronger, might show.

She reminded herself that his sweet words and attentiveness were an exercise, a workout drill that would bring him closer to his ultimate goal of finding a partner, not a lover, friend and wife all wrapped into one.

Leo wished Violet would look at him, allow him to show her he might be boyfriend material. But she kept gazing past him. She was being that fierce, angry panda he so adored, and he wanted to gently swing her face to his, and kiss her. Not an exuberant kiss this time. A real one.

The kind a girlfriend would want.

He was working on opening up his thinking and was realizing that he wanted love, weddings and happily ever afters with someone he understood and enjoyed being around.

Someone like Violet.

Somehow, those popular visions around relationships that he'd never understood all seemed to make sense when he was with her.

"I like that you still believe in love and want a wedding," he said.

She crumpled the paper cup her cider had been in and tossed it in the trash. "Yeah, well, Wyatt doesn't get to destroy me or what I want. He left town, you know. He couldn't take the heat after leaving me at the altar."

"And you stayed."

"I did."

"I think I'd like a wedding. In a church."

She yawned, the angry panda suddenly gone, replaced by exhaustion. "I think I need to go home."

"Want to grab your costume? I'll give you a ride."

He'd parked at the school after driving them in from her place. He'd thought they'd have a bit more time together tonight, mingling during the event, but something was irking Violet and he longed to settle her.

"I'll pick up Dezzie tomorrow when the streets are less busy."

They weaved through the crowds and walked the few blocks to the school.

"Are you ever going to buy a new car?" she asked, waiting for Leo to unlock the doors of his ancient vehicle.

"Yeah."

"When?"

"Probably on the day I feel like my future is unfolding as it should and I can breathe again."

He looked at her over his car's rusty roof. He hoped that day would come soon.

"Good idea, because Christine probably wouldn't be caught dead in this thing." Violet climbed in, patting the dash of the car. "No offense, old girl."

"Yeah, I don't think I'm ever giving her a ride anywhere." He gave a self-deprecating chuckle. "I give up."

"You give up?"

He nodded. "I've realized I want something more than a partnership. Something like what you've described."

He had her attention now. He could feel it zeroing in on him in the small cab. "But you're waiting, right? Until you have lots of money?"

"To start a family? I don't know. I'd still like to be financially secure, as well as have the time to be fully present."

Violet remained quiet, arms crossed, as they drove to the edge of town, then down her driveway. The porch light was on, and he could see Onesie sitting on the railing, waiting for them, his tail flicking back and forth as if they'd been out past the cat's appointed curfew.

"I heard a rumor," Violet said, her voice flat, as he stopped the car.

Leo gripped the steering wheel a little tighter. "Yeah?"

"About a trade."

He swallowed, wishing there was a way to skip this conversation. They were two months out until this season's trading deadline, but his name was on at least one list. He still wasn't sure if that was a good thing or not. In terms of his career, likely good. In terms of him and Violet, not so good.

"I might get moved," he said. He was afraid to be hopeful regarding his time in the league. Trades could be a sign of moving up or of moving down.

"So they're talking about it?"

"There have been discussions." Unless he'd end up close to his family in Montana, he wasn't in favor of being traded. He wanted to settle here in Texas, and specifically in a place closer to Peach Blossom Hollow than San Antonio. A place that was feeling as much like home as much as Montana did.

Violet popped out of his car without a good-bye, moving way too fast to her front door for her mood to be considered calm or okay.

Leo climbed out of the driver's seat slowly, wondering if he'd be invited in, or if she was too angry about the possibility of a trade.

He trailed after her, afraid of how she was re-acting, what she might say and, ultimately, how she might hurt him. Because without realizing quite how he'd gotten to this point, she held his heart and could dash it with a few careless, hurting words.

"I don't think the talks are that serious," he said, coming up the porch steps as she flung open her door, keys bunched in her hand.

Once inside, she kicked off her shoes, and he followed, not removing his boots. If she was going to yell at him, he wanted it to be about something impersonal, such as his footwear.

"They don't mind moving players like me, though. New ones who are unattached. Not yet settled into the city, team, or the like."

Violet's keys thumped down on her kitchen counter with a jangle as she muttered something about a curse. She flung open the fridge door and pulled out a can of root beer. Nothing for him. Not even a bite of her homemade kimchi—an old family recipe she'd wrangled from her mother.

She was upset. Really upset.

"Maybe I should go."

He'd been hoping to kiss her tonight, show her that he was developing feelings for her that he thought might be love, but that idea now looked like a bad one. Or maybe it was good? She'd taught him that sometimes when a woman was upset or mad, she was hurting inside and just needed some kindness. Nice words, a hug, a kiss. Reassurance that she was loved.

"You could be traded anytime in the next eight weeks?" Violet asked.

"Nine."

She turned on the tablet that was sitting on the counter. A photo of her smiling face flashed up, along with what looked like a bio, before she quickly closed the app and opened her calendar.

She jabbed at it with a shaking hand, counting the weeks. "Eight."

"Good. That helps decrease the odds of me being traded." He lifted her hand from the tablet and swiped back to her picture in the first app. "What's this?"

His heart fell as he realized what it was. A dating app. One with a notification icon that blared out the number *ten*. As in ten matches waiting for her to choose from. Or maybe it was ten messages from someone who liked her, who saw the same wonderful potential that Leo did?

Her profile photo was beautiful, her smile bright and sunny. He skimmed her bio. No surprise; it was well-written.

She snatched her tablet away from him and shut it off, then stared at him, jaw jutting as though she was daring him to mention the app.

"I'm not going to laugh at you."

"Good. Because, FYI, I'm on this thing because *you* never bothered to find someone for me."

And he never would. He was starting to realize he'd never intended to. Not to be a jerk, but because so few men, even the top athletes he knew, would ever be good enough to set up with his sweet friend.

"I think it's brave." He gestured to the tablet. "Putting yourself out there."

Her jaw relaxed, and he scooped her hands up in his own. "I'm glad you still want a partner."

"Some of us are looking for *love*."

She pulled away from him, busying herself with her root beer.

"A partner means a friend," he said. "It means laughter and fun. And love, too. It's the whole package. If you find the right person, you can have it all."

"Right!" She looked at him, her face awash with a weak, relieved smile. For a second he thought she was going to kiss him. Then she grew somber. "But *you* don't fall in love."

"I think I just never had the right woman in my life. I'm sure I'll soon learn how to recognize it," he said quietly. He shifted closer and brushed her bangs away from her forehead. "You're such an angry panda tonight. Are you okay?"

She gave him a fiery look, and he chuckled.

"I happen to like that side of you." He tipped his head, angling it so his lips lined up with hers. Violet froze, but she didn't push him away, and he gave her the gentle kiss he'd been thinking about all night.

* * *

Violet couldn't think. She could barely breathe.

Leo was kissing her. Like, for real kissing her. On purpose. With intent.

He leaned away, but she gripped his face between her palms and kissed him back, long and slow.

Best kiss ever.

Maybe the man was coming around, after all.

Wait. What was she thinking?

Her head was all messed up today, with it being her supposed-to-be wedding anniversary, and she was being swayed by desperation, sadness and longing, as well as the way he seemed to be turning his thoughts around regarding romance and love.

He might decide he was open to the idea, but that didn't mean he was going to fall in love with *her*. He could be rebounding after losing the Christine dream, attaching himself to Violet because of the way she was helping his career. He could simply be saying the right things, like she'd taught him to.

Then there was the blaring fact that he was doing well as a rookie and had made it onto a trade list. If he was traded, he'd be leaving. If not this season, possibly the next.

Him kissing her could even be a reaction to the way she was pulling back tonight. His expression when he'd spotted her on the dating app hadn't been a happy one, though he'd said the right things. He'd looked the way she felt about Daisy-Mae slipping away from their friendship, as she fell further and deeper in love.

But the biggest thing—Violet wasn't willing to settle for anything less than love, and still didn't know if he truly understood what she needed. Leo was one giant risk, a man who could be swept far away from her in eight weeks or less.

She broke the kiss and stepped back, shaking her head. "This isn't right. It's not what either of us needs."

"What if it is?"

"I want more than you can give."

"But you're right about partners—the love, friendship, and helping each other. I believe in that. I understand why things didn't work out with Christine now. I was trying to force a stupid partner idea on us, when love and friendship are the foundation a relationship needs."

Violet looked down, wishing he wasn't so darn

perfect. He was always there at the right time, doing and saying the right thing, making her feel seen and adored, his moods leveling out her own.

It would be so easy to say yes.

"Vi?"

"You're a seriously fantastic friend, Leo. But I'm feeling vulnerable tonight." She made sure her voice lacked emotion. "You're saying things you might not understand. Words that mean really deep and important things to me."

He reached for her hand. "I know we'd be great together."

Violet inhaled a deep breath and held it. Her mind was screaming for her to say yes, because they *were* so great together, and it was straight-up awful when they were apart.

"Leo, when I fall, I fall hard. And I can't change our relationship on a whim."

She had it in her to fall in love again, but not to have her heart shattered. It could be broken only so many times before you simply couldn't put it back together again.

"It's not a whim."

"I fear this is nothing more than an opportunistic moment."

"I am *not* 'failing up' like your old date was."

His eyes flashed with that unfamiliar anger. He looked ready to fight her on this.

"You can't just replace the Christine dream with a Violet vision," she said, feeling slightly panicky. She wanted so badly to jump into his arms, but was afraid that what he was offering was different from her hopes.

"I'm not trying to. They're very, very different."

"The stakes are too high to dive into something like this tonight. You need to let me sleep on it. I can't let us fumble over the line, especially if we're both feeling vulnerable right now. Me about Wyatt and the wedding that never was, and you about giving up on Christine."

"I'm not feeling vulnerable."

"You need to leave," she begged, feeling her resolve weaken. "Please. Before we make a mistake that'll ruin our friendship."

Leo stared at her for a long moment, jaw set, eyes flashing.

"Please, Leo. You're too important to me."

When she didn't stand down, he pushed away from the counter. He adjusted his cowboy hat, turned and left, his boots pounding down her front steps, his black jersey fading into the night as he headed to his car.

CHAPTER 10

*L*eo almost wished he was being traded. He couldn't believe Violet had asked him to leave last week after he'd given her the sweetest kiss.

Then she'd kissed him right back, and it had been like floating on air.

Why, if they were such good friends, couldn't she just trust him? What he felt was real, as was everything he'd said. He wanted commitment, friendship, that special something he knew some couples had that ran so deep words weren't even needed, and Violet was his chance to have that.

He was pretty sure she felt it, too, but was scared. Was it because she'd been burned in the past and thought he would break her heart?

Violet was so incredibly easy to be with, and she helped him reach for things he couldn't even see on his own. She tested him and improved him just by being herself. How could that not be love? He thought about her all the time, and at the moment he was grumpy, unfocused, and couldn't sleep.

He was either having a mental breakdown or in love.

Either way, he was going crazy. She'd wanted to sleep on it, but hadn't called or texted the next day. He'd waited. And waited. Nothing. No word. He was giving her space, but it was so damn hard.

And now he feared he'd given her too much space, because a week had passed. He'd had a string of away games, and when he'd finally seen her in the rink's tunnels yesterday, she'd waved and then quickly ducked into her locker room.

There was no way she was still feeling vulnerable after a week, which meant she didn't want to talk about moving from friends to lovers. She was done. Running away from him and not giving him an answer was her answer. It was a polite no thank you.

An answer he really didn't want to accept.

His frustration and inability to fix things made him want to punch something.

The man she was looking for was right here. *Here.*

But he had a plan. Tonight they'd talk, or at least he'd apologize. He was on her turf, one of the bachelors to be auctioned off at the Sweetheart Creek library fundraiser, where he'd help someone with a day of chores.

When he'd signed up, he'd been thinking of Violet. When he'd chosen the shirt for tonight— one she'd told him never to wear when meeting Christine—he'd been thinking of Violet. Now, standing in front of a barn full of women under twinkling lights and Valentine's Day decorations, he thought of Violet.

But he didn't see her anywhere, and he'd been here for thirty minutes. Both Daisy-Mae and the local librarian, Karen, had made it sound as though she was a volunteer. But they hadn't seen her, either. Nobody had.

Which meant the chances were very slim that he was going to be auctioned off to Violet tonight and enjoy a happily ever after.

He supposed, if nothing else, he should be glad he wasn't alone in this misery. Louis Bellmore was standing beside him. Although instead of looking uncomfortable, he was gazing at a woman in the second row, one with wavy brown hair. She caught his eye and smiled, giving a little wave that said all sorts of things in a message meant for Louis, but understood by plenty.

"Are you gaming the system?" Leo asked, turning to the coach. "Is she your girlfriend? Is she bidding on you tonight?" The woman looked familiar, and he was fairly certain she was one of Violet's friends. The one with her arch enemy living next door or something like that.

Louis narrowed his eyes. "Excuse me? Are you accusing me of cheating?"

"Rigging the game, actually."

Louis turned back to the crowd, shoulders straight, fighting a smile. "I don't know what you're talking about."

"Yeah, sure. How long have you been dating?"

"It took a while to convince her."

"So, like, your whole life?"

Louis stared at him for a long moment as though contemplating how much he might be worth in an immediate trade. Leo considered apologizing, but instead squared his own shoulders.

"Mind your own business," Louis muttered.

So Louis had a love life. How had that happened? That joke he and Violet had made a while back about him being in love hadn't actually been jokes…

"It's possible to have a life outside of hockey," Louis added.

"Huh," Leo repeated. "Hey, have you seen Violet?"

"Nope." Louis grinned at the woman in the second row again. The way they were making eyes at each other was almost too much.

"I hope they have barf bags around here," Leo muttered.

He scanned the crowd again, catching the gaze of Mrs. Fisher, the Longhorn Diner's waitress. She was old enough to be his mother and was eagerly waiting for things to begin from her seat in the front row. She gave him a little wave and blew a kiss.

Wasn't she married?

And where was Violet?

* * *

From where Violet was sitting, in the tiny hayloft that served as an office in the town's community events barn, she could see Leo waiting for the bidding to start. The fundraiser had changed since last year. There were no more blind matchups, so you knew who you were bidding on to take care of chores for you. Smart move, because having Louis and Leo standing around, ready to be bid upon, was setting mouths watering.

Violet had cringed when she'd noticed Leo's name on the list of bachelors for tonight. He wasn't going to let her hide from him any longer. And seeing that he was wearing that awful Hawaiian shirt she'd told him was way too bright to be in fashion anywhere on the planet, he was definitely looking for her attention.

Which was fair, and she commended him on using any means possible. She'd been avoiding him since their last kiss, and she held no pride in her general gutlessness. But she was scared.

What if he wasn't actually offering love?

Or what if he was, and then got traded?

What if she was being a big chicken and was about to lose out on the biggest love of her life?

She inhaled a steadying breath and double-checked her clipboard and bachelor tags, knowing she was putting off going down there and seeing Leo.

She needed to take the risk and say yes to him. She could ask to take things slowly, and find out where he truly was with the idea of love and family.

"Who are you bidding on tonight?" Jenny asked, joining Violet in the loft as she collected the fundraiser's cash box. She must have caught something in Violet's expression because she stopped. "What's wrong?"

"Nothing." She held the clipboard closer to her chest. She planned to take a leap and bid on Leo tonight. However, the idea of putting herself out there made her light-headed, and she didn't think discussing it would help. "Are you bidding on Dylan?"

Jenny laughed hard. "Dylan?" she gasped. "No way."

"I thought you two had a little something going on underneath all the fighting."

Jenny's cheeks turned pink, but she continued shaking her head. "He's sweet. Really. But the two of us? I don't think so."

"Why not?"

Jenny shrugged and waved her free hand. "What about you? Daisy-Mae said you were trying a dating app?"

Violet rolled her eyes. "There are a *lot* of fish out in the sea and that's exactly where they're going to stay."

Jenny gave an amused snort of understanding. "Glowing recommendation for me to try the app."

"Truthfully, I haven't gotten past the chat-on-line stage with anyone."

"Slim pickings?"

"I don't know. I was going to meet a few of them in real life, but I sort of lost the heart for it." Mostly because Leo had kissed her and asked for a chance.

And anyway, she was certain none of the men she'd met through the app would be as easy to hang out with as he was. They were also unlikely to have that special something that always brought her out of her shell.

She missed Leo. Everything about him from their quick and easy connection to that ridiculous shirt he was wearing tonight.

And he was down there, right now, waiting for her to give him an answer about moving from friends to lovers.

"Good thing I'm happy alone," Jenny said cheerfully, heading to the top of the stairs.

"No, you're not," Violet called after her.

Realizing she couldn't put off tonight's tasks any longer, Violet left the loft and moved to the front of the barn where the bachelors were milling about. She waved to Hannah, in the second row, and to Mrs. Fisher, who was sitting in front of her, looking eager. She began organizing the men in the order they'd be auctioned off.

When she got to Leo, with trembling hands, she passed him a tag with his bachelor number.

"Hey, Leo." She inhaled, trying to play it cool, to calm her shaking voice. She wanted to smile, to give him some sort of signal, but her brain and body were locking down. What if he said no to her? What if she'd read it all wrong? What if he said yes and then broke her heart? "You'll be up after Louis."

There was no way she could talk about their kiss and possible future as friends or something more right here, right now. She needed to bid on him, win it, then speak with him in private during their day together. Otherwise she could end up smooching with him right here in front of everyone—and she still didn't know exactly what he was promising in terms of a relationship and love. She'd hate to make a fool of herself in front of the town a second time.

"Um, nice shirt." She tried for a dry smile, but was so nervous she couldn't manage it, so kept moving down the line.

She was about to give Louis his tag when Leo caught her arm.

"I miss you," he said, his voice low. "And our

friendship. You're avoiding me, and I'm sorry I've made things weird between us a second time. Please forgive me."

There was nothing to forgive. She went to say as much, but he continued, his mouth so close to her ear that his breath sent shivers down her spine. "I'm sorry if I've hurt you or made you scared, Violet. Truly sorry."

Wait. He was *sorry*?

Was he saying he wanted forgiveness for kissing her, because it hadn't truly meant anything, and that she'd been right to give them a cooling-off period?

"There's nothing to be sorry about. We're friends, right?" she said, her voice catching.

"Friends," he whispered back.

He released her arm and she met his gaze, planning to laugh off the hurt she felt, turn it all into a big joke that would set them on familiar ground once again. But he had bags under his deep blue eyes and his expression was borderline desperate. Her heart beat faster. They were so close, his lips just a breath away.

He missed her.

She missed him.

She wanted a chance with this man.

This man who was in trade talks, and was apologizing for screwing up by kissing her.

She stepped back, feeling cold with his body heat no longer reaching out to her.

"Good luck in the auction," she said, her voice barely working.

She spun to give Louis his tag, planning to move down the line as fast as she could, putting more space between herself and Leo and hopefully making it out of the building before she started crying.

But he grabbed her arm again, gently, but firmly. Leo was staring at her with an intense, commanding look that stopped her short. "We *are* friends, right? Truly? You won't keep avoiding me?"

She lowered her head, knowing that if they were *just* friends, she wouldn't be able to move forward. She'd get stuck right where she was, wishing, hoping, dreaming, crying.

"I want to be friends," she admitted. She missed him. Desperately. But she also loved him as so much more than a friend.

CHAPTER 11

*I*t was March, and Leo didn't even need his fingers to count the number of times he and Violet had hung out since their second kiss, or even last month's auction. Exactly zero.

Not having Violet as a friend made life feel barely worth it. And not having her as a girlfriend was even worse.

How did his apology for the way he'd made things uncomfortable between them turn into him agreeing to be nothing more than friends? He'd wanted the night of the auction to go a different way altogether.

He'd thought it smart to apologize, because he'd made her uncomfortable, but then suddenly the conversation was over and he was still in the friend zone. He hadn't even had a chance to share his I'd-be-a-great-boyfriend argument with her.

And she hadn't bid on him, either. Instead he'd spent a long day landscaping for Mrs. Fisher and her husband. Which hadn't been too bad, but it sure didn't rate as high as spending time with Violet.

She wanted to be friends, and he should respect that.

And yet, deep down inside, he felt she was avoiding him because she was scared. From her perspective he had a lot of checkmarks on her don't-date-him list, and she'd had her heart broken enough times to be extra cautious.

But he wasn't going to give up on her until he'd had a chance to argue his case one more time.

And he hoped today's wedding would help him get around Violet's very serious defense system.

Today he'd tell her the truth about how he felt about her.

And maybe, if he was lucky, she would be willing to try one more time when it came to finding the love of her life.

* * *

Violet inhaled the salty air coming in through the window of the pink cottage along the ocean shore in Indigo Bay, South Carolina. The white curtains billowed in the breeze as she set down the curling iron.

"You're a beautiful bride," she said to Daisy-Mae. Her eyes filled with tears, as did her friend's.

Daisy-Mae quickly dabbed a finger under her lashes, trying to collect the tears before they ruined her carefully applied makeup. "You're making me cry!"

Violet scrambled to collect tissues, passing her a handful. "I can't believe you're getting married."

Daisy-Mae's watery smile filled with happiness. "I know. Me, either."

"I predicted this back in September!"

"I totally didn't believe you."

"I know." Violet had lost track of when the fake relationship had become real for Daisy-Mae and Maverick, but was elated her friend was getting the man she'd crushed on for so many years.

"Things are good. No, *more* than good."

"I'm so glad."

"How about you? You haven't been yourself lately."

"Oh. I'm fine." Violet waved her off.

"What did I miss?" Daisy-Mae grabbed Violet's hands, holding them as she peered at her, searching for the truth.

"Nothing," she insisted. "You've been busy falling in love and getting engaged in the most public way possible." Violet laughed. "Trend alert. Daisy-Mae is in the house!"

Her friend looked heavenward and sighed. "Who knew I'd be the one to suggest eloping?"

"All is wrong with the world: Daisy-Mae is willing to elope!" Violet teased.

Eager to get them moving toward the beach for the small, private ceremony, she started to pull her hands away, but her friend tightened her grip.

"Maverick's witness is Leo."

"I know," Violet replied lightly. She'd heard that Brant Wylder, who'd set up Leo with an older rescued dog, was dog-sitting so Leo could come to the Indigo Bay beach wedding between game nights. It was a whirlwind, hush-hush trip, Maverick and Daisy-Mae so eager to wed that they were eloping. But they needed two witnesses. Violet was one, and for some reason Maverick had wrangled Leo to come as the second.

However, the need for witnesses turned out to

be a mistake. It was North Carolina, not South Carolina where they needed wedding witnesses, but by then the tickets had been purchased for Indigo Bay, South Carolina and everyone was ready to go. Violet's slightly superstitious side felt that it was all a sign—especially with having Leo as the other witness.

But most of all, it was an opportunity for her to get brave and tell him how she really felt about him. She just hoped she wouldn't chicken out, or that Leo didn't shatter her heart, because her control was already long gone when it came to him.

"I tried to convince Mav to ask someone else, because I know you two are going through something, but everyone's so crazy busy. Dak's on his honeymoon, the Wylder men have calving or spring football or who knows what, etcetera, etcetera. You get the point."

"It's fine, really."

"Are you sure?" Daisy-Mae asked.

"Yes. Certain. Thank you for inviting him."

"You're up to something."

"No. Yes." She sighed.

"You love him!"

"No!" Violet covered her face. "I mean…"

"Tell me how he makes you feel."

"It's like you're standing at a cocktail party all alone with a drink in your hand. You join a conversation, but you don't know what everyone's laughing about. Then *he* comes along and suddenly you're comfortable and laughing and a part of things. But now he's gone again and I'm back at the party standing there awkwardly, hoping somebody will include me and it'll all turn into fun again."

Daisy-Mae sighed, her expression full of sympathy and confusion. "Oh, hon."

"It'll be fine." She'd checked the NHL trade lists that morning. The deadline had officially passed and Leo was with the Dragons for the time being. That gave them time. Time to figure things out before she once again faced the gut-wrenching fear that he might get traded away from her.

"Come on," she said, feeling nervous. She hurried toward the door and held it open. "The bride can't be late or the groom'll start panicking."

Daisy-Mae, in her flowing white sundress and flowered crown, stopped on the threshold and gave Violet a long hug. "It'll all work out. I promise."

"I know, and I'm fine."

"I want to see you happy."

"Thanks."

They shared a smile and Daisy-Mae stepped out onto the veranda, arms raised as she sucked in a deep breath. "This is it. The day I've been waiting for!" She turned and did a little dance as she squealed in excitement, scaring a small yellow bird off the railing.

With a grin, Violet hooked her arm through her friend's, leading her down the sandy seashell path. "Come on, Daise! Let's go lock this man in."

And, hopefully, by night's end, she'd have Leo locked in as her new boyfriend, as well.

* * *

Leo stood as Daisy-Mae and Violet came across the sugary sand, the breeze toying with the hems of their dresses. Maverick was already standing under the rose-covered archway, waiting for his bride. The wedding was casual, and Leo, as a witness, was to sit in one of two chairs set out in the sand.

Two chairs. Spaced a half foot apart.

Leo edged the chairs closer together and waited for the women to arrive.

Violet was smiling, arm in arm with her best friend. She looked happy. Free.

One word: heart-stoppingly beautiful.

Again, he needed more than one word to describe the woman.

The women hugged, and Violet came to stand on the far side of the second chair. She didn't look at him, and surreptitiously edged her chair farther from his before she sat down.

Leo, pretending to steady his chair in the soft sand, moved it closer again before he sat.

"Hi."

"Hey," she said, her hands twisted in her lap, her gaze solidly on the couple under the archway.

She was wearing what he thought of as an angry panda outfit. It was a white-and-black, half-sleeve sundress with a skirt that grazed her knees, and a giant pink flower splashed across her waistline, the petals flowing out from her right hip. Her hair was in an up-do, with tiny pink roses tucked into the folds, her bangs nearly brushing her lashes. She was gorgeous.

She was biting her lower lip as if nervous that the bride was going to run off or do something equally crazy, and she was still avoiding looking at him. He'd love to believe he was simply too handsome, and she was fearing self-combustion if she dared look at him.

Either way, it made it difficult to start a conversation about the two of them.

"The wedding is up there," she said calmly, raising a finger to point to the couple.

Leo shifted and reached inside his jacket pocket, then held out his palm in front of Violet. On it rested a homemade peach muffin wrapped in plastic and a folded piece of paper. "I was going to make you a cobbler, but I thought a muffin might travel better."

Violet blinked at the offering, then wordlessly, slowly accepted it. Her cheeks were pink and she looked like she was having trouble breathing. He pointed to the square of paper. "This is a list of good cars and salesmen who won't rip you off if you still need to upgrade. But if you'd like, I'll come with you."

Violet blinked again and swallowed. "That would be really nice," she whispered.

The ceremony began, and already tears were leaking down Violet's cheeks, but Leo had a feeling they were more about him than the wedding. He shifted in his chair to wipe them away.

She looked at him, her chin trembling. "I'm scared. But I want…" Her voice broke and she glanced back at the flowery archway.

He knew this wasn't the time or place to have

this conversation, but he desperately wanted to hear what else she had to say. He caressed her cheek with his knuckle, then slid one arm across the back of her chair, angling his upper body so her shoulder fitted against his chest.

"I want you and love," she breathed. "And I don't know if…"

"If I can fall in love?"

She bobbed her head.

"Vi, the past few months without you in my life have been the hardest I've ever endured. I think about you all the time. I miss our laughter and conversations. I keep thinking about things we should do together, and I check my phone a million times a day hoping there's a message from you."

Those tears weren't stopping, but neither was he. "I want a lot more of those kisses we shared. I meant it when I said I think friendship and love are the best foundation for a relationship. And you and me? I believe we have both of those things. I believe we can go the distance."

"Oh, Leo." Her breath hitched, and her eyes filled with something that fueled his hope.

"I know I don't have everything that I'd like to offer you when it comes to a life together. My career is unstable, and I know I could get traded next year. The only thing certain in my life is my desire for you."

* * *

Leo.

How had she ever missed seeing his affection? It was right there, written on his face. His right words and actions were *her* right words and actions. That's why they hadn't worked with Christine. They were Violet's, and had been all along.

She'd let her own fears block her from seeing what was in front of her—a man who loved her.

Speechless, she swiped at her tears before Leo could. She'd planned to be the one arguing her case for love at some point today, and here he was, stunning her. Violet didn't know what to say, how to react other than to kiss him.

Would that be an acceptable reply?

His chair was nestled up to hers, his arm across the back. He was caressing her shoulder in a gentle, soothing motion and she shivered as something raw ran through her nervous system.

He was beautifully turned out for the casual beach wedding in tan linen trousers, the hems rolled up, leather flip-flops and a loose-fitting cotton shirt and suit jacket. Everything looking as though it had been cut to hang magnificently off his muscled shoulders, torso, hips and legs. She'd never seen him look more handsome, and she took a mental picture to save for later.

"I'm praying you still have enough hope in that wounded heart of yours that you'd be willing to give a man like me a chance," Leo said. "That you'll let me try to be your heart's superglue."

"I want more than a year."

"A year is only a start."

"What if we need more time?"

"If things are good and I'm traded, you move with me. Or I quit."

"Quit the NHL?"

He'd do that for her? The man was insane. Intense. Committed and half crazy.

Or really and truly in love.

Or crazy. But maybe love and crazy were actually the same thing.

The woman performing the marriage ceremony cast a warning look Violet's way after her outburst, while Maverick and Daisy-Mae, oblivious to the fact that their witnesses weren't paying attention, continued to smile at each other.

"You know what you want, Violet. And I trust that about you. You've taught me so much about love over the past few months. So…" Leo took her hand in his. "I'm stepping off that cliff right now, hoping the air will catch me."

"You don't need the air to catch you," Violet said, her eyes welling up again. "You've got me above the rocks, waiting with my arms open."

She tilted her body, leaning against his chest as he angled in for a kiss.

"I think I love you, Violet Granger."

"I think I love you, too, Leo Pattra."

The kiss started off sweet. And maybe it was the magic of the wedding, the sunshine, or the sound of the gulls playing above the ocean waves that made this kiss feel different than anything she'd ever experienced.

Or maybe it was Leo.

Maybe it was love.

And maybe, just maybe, that pesky curse that had been plaguing her family's matriarchal line was finally being broken and dissolved by a love much stronger than some bad juju.

Leo shifted closer, his right hand cradling her jaw as he deepened the kiss. She pressed her hands to his chest, wishing to be closer. The kiss stole her breath, and she forgot her surroundings.

The man was magic. That's what it was. It

wasn't the atmosphere or anything else; it was him. Their friendship. Their growing love.

She didn't need to change to be with someone who truly loved her, because he saw her flaws and believed they were beautiful strengths.

EPILOGUE

$\mathcal{V}$iolet pushed on the locker room door, angling her costume's head so she could see better. A cold drink of water right now would be bliss. The door swung open, and she stumbled over the threshold, tumbling into the room. Hands gripped her, righting her again.

"We've got to stop meeting like this."

She knew that deep voice. Violet lifted the dragon head and grinned at Leo. "Where's the fun in that?" she asked.

He planted a kiss on her lips. "I still remember the day I met you. You fell for me, if I recall correctly. It seems to be a habit of yours."

Violet laughed and rolled her eyes. "You also have a habit of being very charming."

"And flattering. You like hearing sweet words, don't you?"

"I do."

"But not as much as you like my kisses."

She smiled.

"I believe I told you when we met that you have a pretty face."

"You did, and I do."

"Is that a hint?"

"Is what a hint?"

"Replying 'I do' twice in a row like that?"

"What? I did? No. Are you…?" She frowned, realizing a few things were off with this situation. "How are you even in here already?" He was still in his hockey gear, but was supposed to be in the post-game meeting in the players' locker room. And where was Daisy-Mae? She should have caught up with Violet by now to help her out of her costume.

"Would you like me to?" Leo asked, eyebrows raised.

"Do what?" She leaned to the right, trying to look over his shoulder into the room, but Leo gently guided her chin so she had to gaze at him.

"Propose?"

"*Propose?*" They'd been dating for only two

275

months, inseparable since Indigo Bay, the wedding and their short scuba diving trip.

But wasn't it a bit quick to get engaged?

Yes, she already knew he was the one. She loved him and knew she'd follow him if he got traded this season. He'd become that important in her life and she'd learned that they actually wanted the same things. Well, except she didn't need a million or two in the bank to feel secure enough to start a family, but she was working on him about that.

She glanced around her locker room, and this time he didn't stop her. Late-season peach blossoms were strewn everywhere, as well as candles. It smelled nice. A lot better than the room normally did.

"What is this?" she asked, barely able to breathe.

"It's too soon, isn't it?"

She nodded, then shook her head. "Not too soon to get engaged. Too soon to get married. We'll need a date at least eighteen months to two years out."

"That long?" She heard the surprise in Leo's voice. "But...didn't you hear about the big deal I've sealed with Family Zone? I'm financially ready for all of this."

It was true that his career was looking better with each passing day, and he was carefully setting up investments, preparing for his future, his retirement, his family.

But to get engaged at this point in his life was still a big step for him. She also knew it wasn't a step he'd take lightly. Only if he was ready.

Her heart swelled.

"Wait. Did I just say yes? You haven't even asked me properly!"

He got down on one knee. "Then I'll ask you now. Violet Granger, the woman who taught me so much about love. Will you marry me? Be my romantic partner who sticks with me through thick and thin, and tells me off in her sweet, angry panda way?"

"I can't believe you worked 'angry panda' into your proposal. Why don't you talk about your belt buckles, too?"

"What do you think I'm giving you as a ring? Untraditional, I know...but they *are* pretty awesome."

She stared at him for a long moment, unsure if he was being serious or not. She really didn't want a belt buckle.

Grinning, Leo pulled something out of one of

his long, knitted hockey socks. A ring box. She let out a breath of relief.

"Apparently I am traditional, after all." He grinned. "Will you take this gift as a token and symbol of my unending love?" He opened the box and revealed the most beautiful, intricate ring she'd ever seen. She reached for it, but her dragon hands were too big and fuzzy to be of any use. "Argh! Get me out of this costume!"

Leo laughed. "Is that a yes?"

"Yes! Yes! Get that ring on my finger now, buster."

He unzipped her costume, and she shrugged it off her shoulders and arms, her left hand extended as soon as it was free. "Ring me, Leo."

He complied, sliding the gorgeous yellow-gold band with its tiny sculpted floral design onto her finger. It was beautiful. Perfect. She gave a little squeal and danced, nearly tripping over her discarded costume.

"Did I ever tell you that you're the best?" She threw her arms around his shoulders.

"Maybe. Better tell me again to see if it rings any bells."

But before she could, he kissed her long and slow, a promise of all the beautiful things still to come in their life.

"Vi?"

"Hmm?"

"One word."

"What?"

"If I had only one word to describe you and this moment, it would be *love*."

She laughed, her heart bursting with happiness. Maybe it hadn't been a curse that had plagued her all these years. Maybe it had actually been a guardian angel of true love sitting on her shoulder, helping to bring her to where she was today—in love with the man she knew without a single doubt that she'd spend the rest of her days with, enjoying all the wonderful moments that true love would bring them in Peach Blossom Hollow.

EPILOGUE PART 2

ack in December…

Louis Bellmore believed in second chances. However, he didn't quite know what to think of the multitude of second chances the universe had been delivering to him recently. His gratitude overflowed not just for the new NHL team, the Dragons, of which he was head coach. But because the team's owner, Miranda Fairchild, was all about second chances for him, for the players and their careers. Including one of his favorite players of all time, and his team captain, Maverick Blades.

Louis had a chance to give these players a re-vitalized career, and as a bonus, he was just a short drive from his hometown of Sweetheart Creek and his family and friends.

And sure, there was a lot of work to do with the Dragons. They were a new NHL team, and weren't exactly doing amazing, but as the season progressed, so did they. They'd actually secured a W or two and were gaining fans.

He was blessed with a job he loved.

And not only that, but a steal of a deal had come up on a house in the town he'd grown up in. He now lived right next door to what had been the Hopewells' cabin, set on Cherry Lane in good ol' Sweetheart Creek.

That meant he was minutes away from the town's tiny grass airstrip. And as luck would have it, a hanger for his new Cessna had become available. Better yet, there was a noncommercial air-port close to the Dragons' arena, meaning he could literally fly to work. Two passions satisfied, and living in a town that felt like family.

But even sweeter was that his little piece of real estate had landed him as a next-door neighbor to Hannah Murphy, the woman he'd crushed on as a teenager. And yeah, this might be where his lucky streak ran out, because she was certain to recall all the ways that his straightforward style, which worked beautifully as an NHL coach, hadn't done much for her sweet and gentle spirit. As a teen she'd had her entire life planned out, centered around a man Louis had always felt wasn't quite enough for her.

And now, for the first time since she was a teen, Hannah was single again and living right next door. Louis didn't even have to make an excuse to bump into her. All he had to do was convince Hannah that instead of being enemies, they should be friends.

And then, maybe not so long after that, more than friends.

Easy, right?

HOCKEY SWEETHEARTS: HAVE YOU READ THEM ALL?

The Cupcake Cottage

Peach Blossom Hollow

Chocolate Cherry Cabin

The Peppermint Lodge

Sugar Cookie Country House

The Huckleberry Bookshop

The Gingerbread Cafe

There are two more series set in Sweetheart Creek!

The Cowboys of Sweetheart Creek, Texas

The Cowboy's Stolen Heart (Levi)

The Cowboy's Secret Wish (Myles)

The Cowboy's Second Chance (Ryan)

The Cowboy's Sweet Elopement (Brant)

The Cowboy's Surprise Return (Cole)

Indigo Bay

Sweet Matchmaker (Ginger and Logan)

Sweet Holiday Surprise (Cash & Alexa)

Sweet Forgiveness (Ashton & Zoe)

Sweet Troublemaker (Nick & Polly)

Sweet Joymaker (Maria & Clint)

MORE SMALL TOWN ROMANCES BY JEAN ORAM...

Veils and Vows

The Promise (Book 0: Devon & Olivia)

The Surprise Wedding (Book 1: Devon & Olivia)

A Pinch of Commitment (Book 2: Ethan & Lily)

The Wedding Plan (Book 3: Luke & Emma)

Accidentally Married (Book 4: Burke & Jill)

The Marriage Pledge (Book 5: Moe & Amy)

Mail Order Soulmate (Book 6: Zach & Catherine)

Blueberry Springs

Whiskey and Gumdrops (Mandy & Frankie)

Rum and Raindrops (Jen & Rob)

Eggnog and Candy Canes (Katie & Nash)

Sweet Treats (3 short stories—Mandy, Amber, & Nicola)

Vodka and Chocolate Drops (Amber & Scott)

Tequila and Candy Drops (Nicola & Todd)

Champagne and Lemon Drops (Beth & Oz)

ACKNOWLEDGMENTS

A special thank you goes to Nate for naming Leo for me. Also for coming up with the meet cute for this story. He suggested the scene where Leo and Violet met, but wasn't super impressed with my version of it. I guess it didn't match up with what he had envisioned in his imagination. He did say I could use his idea including Leo saying, "You have a pretty face."

For those who found the wooing tips that Violet teaches Leo intriguing, these are based off of the love languages that are described much more fully in Gary Chapman's book *The Five Love Languages*.

Thanks to my editor Margaret, my beta reader team, my error team and my Jeansters.

ABOUT THE AUTHOR

 Jean Oram is a *New York Times* and *USA Today* best-selling romance author. Inspiration for her small town series came from her own upbringing on the Canadian prairies. Although, so far, none of her characters have grown up in an old schoolhouse or worked on a bee farm. Jean still lives on the prairie with her husband, two kids, and big shaggy dog where she can be found out playing in the snow or hiking.

Become an Official Fan:
www.facebook.com/groups/jeanoramfans

Newsletter: www.jeanoram.com/signup
Website & blog: www.jeanoram.com

Find a complete, up-to-date book list at:
www.jeanoram.com/books